Something was not quite right, Jake thought

Who was she? Why did Dana stir such feelings in him? How did she know such things about his past? There was something about her that evoked memories and feelings in him in a way that was both painful and yet extraordinarily joyful.

She made him remember what it was like to savor being alive. Yet she made him sad at times because she was a reminder of how sterile his life had become.

How many attractive women had walked in front of him and he hadn't even noticed them? Well, he was noticing now.

He had to see her again.

Regan Forest has been very busy over the past year! She's a newlywed who claims to have had her own storybook romance. Everything she writes about has come true for herself. Well, maybe not the part about dragons and ghosts, but certainly true love and happy endings. Regan makes her home in Arizona and enjoys writing about the unusual—as you'll find out in *The Sheriff of Devil's Fork*. Here, the heroine inherits a little more than she was expecting!

Books by Regan Forest

THE SHERIFF OF DEVIL'S FORK

REGAN FOREST

Harlequin Books

TORONTO • NEW YORK • LONDON
AMSTERDAM • PARIS • SYDNEY • HAMBURG
STOCKHOLM • ATHENS • TOKYO • MILAN
MADRID • WARSAW • BUDAPEST • AUCKLAND

For Heidi, with love

Special thanks to Tom Grau for sharing part of his childhood

Published October 1993

ISBN 0-373-25564-0

THE SHERIFF OF DEVIL'S FORK

Printed in U.S.A.

1

IT WAS RAINING HARD when Sheriff Jake MacGuire ducked into his pickup to answer the radio summons.

"Yeah?" he barked impatiently into the receiver.

"Where are you?" asked the voice of Henry Wilcox from the switchboard at the county jail.

Through the streaked front windshield, Jake watched rain pelt down on the tombstones and drip from the branches over the graves. It was none of Henry's business where he was. "I'm off duty. This call had better be important."

Henry, who was well acquainted with the sheriff's bad temper, was silent a moment before he answered diffidently. "The ham thief has struck again. Viola Hollaman is missing a ham from her refrigerator. The thief broke in through the kitchen window."

Jake suppressed an oath. He wasn't in the mood for this. He didn't even want to think about the bizarre series of thefts in Devil's Fork. "Call Fargo and tell him to take care of it."

"He's at his family picnic. You know that."

"They won't be having a picnic in this weather."

"The picnic was moved to the church basement. It's a family *reunion*, Sheriff. Viola Hollaman is hysterical. The lock on her kitchen window is broken and she's afraid the thief will come back because she has another ham in the freezer."

Rainwater dripped from Jake's dark hair onto his forehead and down his cheeks. His shoulders were wet. If the thief was stupid enough to strike in the pouring rain on a Sunday afternoon, maybe he was also stupid enough to leave tracks in the mud around Viola's farmhouse. "Tell Viola I'm on my way," he growled.

Jake did not start the engine at once, but sat a few moments longer looking out through the rain-streaked window. The tombstones on the green expanse of lawn looked lonely in the mist. Just as they looked lonely in autumn covered with frost, and in winter covered with snow. And in spring when the winds whipped through the greening branches. And now during a summer storm that washed away the soft layer of blossoms that had floated down from the honeysuckle trees.

The flowers he had left on one of the graves drooped with the weight of the rain. It didn't matter; their message remained: *No one deserves a grave without flowers. Even though you wanted to leave me, I will always remember the good times.* Jake looked up at the dark sky with eyes of steel. *Someday . . .* he vowed for the thousandth time in seven years. Someday he was going to discover the identity of the man who ran away with his wife and then left the scene of the crash that killed her.

The county roads were running like rivers, and it took Jake thirteen minutes to reach the Hollaman farm. On the front porch, behind a veil of water falling from the overflowing roof gutters, stood the widow Hollaman and a handful of her neighbors.

The squeak of the pickup's door could be heard over the sound of the pouring rain. Jake stepped out and his boots sank into inches of mud.

Viola was wide-eyed and wringing her hands. "Sheriff MacGuire!" she said as he walked up her porch steps. "We aren't safe in our own houses anymore!"

He knew it would do no good to point out to her that the ham thief had never harmed anyone. But it was true these ham thefts were the town's worst crime spree in decades. Normally Devil's Fork was a peaceful rural Colorado community, where citizens slept soundly in their beds at night.

Jake looked down from his six-foot height at the elderly woman, ignoring the excited exclamations of her neighbors. "Nothing else taken?"

"No. Just the ham from the bottom shelf of the ice box."

"When did you buy the ham?"

"Yesterday. I was going to have the Gillans over for dinner."

"Where?"

"Why, here, of course, in the dining room."

Jake strove for patience. "Where did you buy the ham?"

"Oh. At the First Street Market. Why?"

"Did you notice anybody suspicious hanging around the meat counter?"

"There were several people there, some friendly talk, you know how it is. I can't remember seeing anybody suspicious, no. You think that's how the thief knows who has hams?"

The lawman nodded. "Did you hear a car in your drive?"

"No. I was taking my nap. But I asked the neighbors already. Nobody saw any car." She looked up at him as if she were ready to cry. "The villain jimmied the lock and climbed in through my kitchen window!"

This is getting more serious, Jake thought. It was the first actual break-in by the thief; the other three times he had merely walked in through unlocked doors. Jake kicked off his muddy boots at the doorstep and followed Viola inside.

He saw muddy footprints on the floor. "Stocking feet," he said. "The thief took off his shoes."

"Oh, my!" Viola exclaimed. "He'll catch his death running around in the rain in his stocking feet!"

Jake, on his knees where he was examining the prints, looked at her incredulously.

He checked the window and asked for her late husband's toolbox. He was at work fixing the lock when Matthew Beavers, Viola's neighbor, rushed into the kitchen.

"I saw the police truck," the swarthy dark-haired man said, panting. "Wondered what was wrong. So! The ham thief again. What is it—a dozen break-ins now? Meadowlark County's no longer safe to live in, Sheriff."

Leaning over the windowsill, Jake said coolly, "You complaining about the way I do my job, Beavers?"

Matthew Beavers's shoulders sagged. "I'm just saying people are mighty concerned."

The sheriff turned cold pale eyes on him, a look the people of Devil's Fork knew well and dreaded. Beavers backed away as if there was a gun to his chest. Jake's voice was soft and threatening. "You're tracking mud all over Viola's house, Beavers. Look at that! Tracks all the way from the front door. What the *hell* do you think you're doing walking in here in those muddy boots?"

Beavers flushed angrily. "Shouldn't you be more concerned with the heinous crime at hand than—"

Jake silenced him with his eyes. "Take off your boots."

"I ain't gonna take—"

"I said take off your boots."

Beaver's face turned bright red. His fists tightened. "Nobody talks to me like—"

"Either take them off or you're under arrest."

Viola let out a horrified shriek. "Sheriff, it's all right! I can clean the floor!"

"This is abuse of the law!" the man protested weakly. By this time his back was tight against the wall, although Jake hadn't moved an inch toward him.

Jake stared him down, waiting, aware that neighbors had ventured inside and were congregated at the kitchen door, watching. Matthew Beavers was fighting for his dignity. Jake was fighting to control his temper. He didn't like insolence.

Glancing toward the crowd—four women and three other men whose Sunday afternoon had been enlivened considerably, he raised his voice. "I want all of you men—starting with Beavers here—to remove your boots." He turned to the man by the wall and scowled. "Are you going to stop wasting my time?"

Viola Hollaman began to sniffle. "The others all wiped their feet, Sheriff. . . ."

Jake laid his hand protectively on her thin shoulder. "Viola, whoever broke in must have approached the house on foot. He either had a vehicle parked some distance away and hiked over here in the pouring rain, or else he lives close by." He looked at Beavers and then at the others. "If any man here refuses to remove his boots, it might just be because his socks are covered with mud. Now, Beavers, if you want to continue to interfere with a police investigation . . ."

JAKE'S MOOD was foul as he pulled up in front of the Prairie Chicken Saloon. No suspect had emerged; Viola's neighbors all had passably clean socks. He decided he needed a volunteer to hang around the First Street Market meat counter. But hell, this was Sunday night. He'd worry about setting a trap for the ham thief next week.

The usual Sunday cars were parked outside the Prairie Chicken—the black Buick his cousin had just bought; Nellie Jean Schrock's gray Plymouth; the preacher's motorcycle, covered with a plastic sheet to protect it from the rain.

Inside, the floor of the saloon was covered with muddy boot and paw prints. Two dogs were lying under tables; another was walking lazily around, seeking companionship. The guitar player, Preacher Donald Whitney, was crooning a melancholy country ballad. The music hurt and felt good at the same time—the way kneading a cramped muscle felt good and also hurt. Jake's clothes were too damp to be comfortable, but he eased into his usual Sunday-night place at the bar next to his cousin, Russell MacGuire, who was the mayor of Devil's Fork. He reached down to pet the wandering dog, a black Labrador, muttering, "Hello, Brutus," then hunched over the bar and ordered a beer. Although he was not wearing his badge, his pistol hung in a holster at his hip because he was always on call.

Russell grinned at him. "You been out walking in the rain, Cousin?"

"I've been on a call. The ham thief struck at Viola Hollaman's farm."

"What the hell is with this nut? Walks into houses and takes hams out of refrigerators! What are you going to do about it, Jake? People in other towns are starting to hear about it, thanks to our overzealous newspaper editor. We're becoming a laughingstock." He banged a fist on the table. "I won't have *my* town made a laughingstock! The town's image is my image."

The lawman drank thirstily from his mug of cold beer. "I'll take care of it," he promised impatiently.

"How?"

"Never mind how. You stick to worrying. I'll do the work."

The blond young mayor, dressed in dark slacks, a pale lavender shirt and cowboy boots, motioned for another drink. "Okay, okay. I've got more important things to discuss, anyhow. There's no money in the town treasury to finish paying for the swimming pool, and the committee wants our construction company to float the loan."

"What do you mean 'our' company, Russ? Since you bought me out, the business is your headache, not mine."

"You still own stock. If I go bankrupt we both lose."

Jake wiped his mouth with the back of his hand. "I told you before you contracted for the pool that I thought the company would run into trouble getting paid. Hell, you're the mayor. You knew the financial situation. If you hadn't spent the entire city budget on that dog statue, we wouldn't be in this mess."

Russell bristled. "That dog statue, as you call it, is the most important single accomplishment of any mayor in the history of this town. A monument to the spirit of our pioneer founders. It was a MacGuire, don't forget, who owned that hero dog."

Jake laughed. "I hardly think that justifies having the man who's petting the dog look just like you."

"Why not me? I'm the one responsible for the statue, aren't I? I don't want anybody forgetting it."

"No one ever will, Russ, not with your likeness in stone dominating the town square. It's what broke us, and everybody knows it."

"Everybody is proud as hell of that statue."

Jake grinned. "I'll admit that's true. I'm proud of it myself."

The mayor laughed and reached down to stroke the Labrador's head. "The town has the money on paper. All we have to do is collect the back taxes on Maude O'Connor's house. What Maude's estate owes us will more than cover the municipal-pool balance."

Tax collection. So that was it. Russ was throwing it in *his* lap. Jake, like the rest of the city, had long forgotten that outstanding tax bill. But he should have expected this from Russ. Jake leaned his elbows on the bar and drank steadily. He was a good-looking man, taller than his cousin. At thirty-four, he was two years younger than Russell, but looked older. Both were eligible bachelors, now that Russell was divorced, but they didn't compete for women. Russell, the friendly, extroverted politician, was linked romantically with two women at the moment, and Jake with none. Most members of the small community considered Jake sullen and unsociable. The challenge of breaking down the sheriff's defensive barriers was a subject the local women often discussed behind closed doors. Unmarried women, convinced he was not over the bitterness of his wife's betrayal, watched Jake's every move. He knew it and didn't like it.

"Did Maude O'Connor have a will?" Jake asked. "Has somebody inherited the house?"

"Yeah. Maude left everything to a relative in Dallas, but the heir hasn't been notified yet, because the will was only found yesterday. You can bill the heir on notification."

Jake shrugged unenthusiastically. "What makes you think some Texan is going to pay us that kind of money? The heir will put the house up for sale for the taxes, but I don't know how they'll sell it. Who the hell would buy that property? There's something strange about that house."

"Yeah." Russell nodded thoughtfully. "Something damned strange. I've heard it's haunted. Do you still believe in ghosts, Cuz?"

"I never did believe in ghosts."

"Beg to argue there. Remember Granny Inez's attic?"

Jake burst into laughter. "You were the one who was scared of Granny's attic."

"Well, hell, yeah, after you told me a headless ghost lived up there!" He shuddered with the long-ago memory. "What about the O'Connor house? You ever been in there?"

"We both have. When we were kids. Don't you remember going with Granny Inez to see Mrs. O'Connor—when she was the third-grade teacher? We got scolded for running up the stairs and sliding down the banister while Maude and Inez were busy with the business of the Ladies' Club."

Russell smiled. "Oh, man! The Ladies' Club! Those conniving old biddies controlled Devil's Fork for years. Well, Maude O'Connor was the last of them."

Jake chuckled. "What I remember is a bunch of old girls sitting around playing bridge and exchanging recipes and gossip."

"Acting innocent was their cover. They had enough dirt to blackmail every individual in the mayor's office, if it served their purpose. Make no mistake, old buddy, they ran this town, all right." He tipped up his beer mug, took a long drink and set it down angrily. "We never want another organization like that to get started here. No women taking over the running of my town. You and I can do that job just dandy."

Jake scowled. "You'd better make that beer your last before you get any louder. People wouldn't appreciate hearing their good-buddy mayor spouting off like a feudal lord."

Both men glanced around to see who was within earshot. The customers at the bar were all listening to Preacher Whitney, who sat on a raised platform strumming his guitar. He was wearing boots and jeans, with a clerical collar under his plaid shirt. At one end of the bar, in her usual place, sat Nellie Jean Schrock, sipping cola and lime. In her gray slacks and starched white shirt the thirty-five-year-old spinster looked like a bird perched on the bar stool. Her eyes were fixed on the singing preacher, her concentration so deep she was unaware of anyone else in the place.

Jake brushed his wet hair back from his forehead. The Preacher was singing about waking in the morning with a woman who was a stranger and remembering the little wife back home. Jake listened for a time, reflecting on the song, wondering where Donald got his inspiration. From townspeople he knew about? No one else seemed the least concerned that Donald's songs were as unpreacherlike as his loud motorcycle. Or that the preacher hadn't asked Nellie Jean Schrock to marry him yet, even though the two were considered a couple. Sometimes Jake was astounded by the eccentricities of people in the town of his birth. The place seemed to get more illogical, not less, through the years, and Jake MacGuire felt misplaced in the middle of it. Devil's Fork was a town that had grown from a discovery of gold that turned out to be fool's gold—fool's gold dug up from the river mud by a dog named Brutus. It must have been a forecast of the town's personality. "Is that a song the preacher wrote himself?" he asked his cousin now.

Russell nodded. "Yeah, he's damn good at writing songs. And what a voice the guy's got. If you'd ever go to church you'd know that the entire congregation cries when Donald sings 'Amazing Grace' at the end of his Sunday-morning sermons. I suppose it's no wonder Nellie Jean goes into trance when Donald turns on that nasal twang."

The preacher began to croon another song about unfaithfulness—a lousy theme for a preacher, Jake thought. This one sent him plunging into the doldrums. Everybody in town knew that his wife had been with another man that night seven years ago when her car flipped over on the ice. The man had disappeared and Jake had fantasized about killing him ever since. The song and the rain reminded him how lonely he was, and he didn't like to be reminded. He tried to keep too busy to be lonely by holding down two jobs, but Devil's Fork was such a quiet community the work still didn't keep him busy enough. He spent time alone walking in the fields with his dogs or riding his horse along the river, and at night he did the accounting work for his job as tax assessor. Sometimes he found himself in the Prairie Chicken Saloon, though he didn't make a habit of staying long.

Russell nudged his arm and drew his attention to the loud voices at one of the tables. An argument was getting profane. A chair went crashing to the floor as two men rose, yelling at each other.

"Nobody insults my dog and gets away with it!"

"I said your mutt couldn't track a grouse if it landed on his back! You gonna stop me from telling the truth?"

"I'm gonna stop you from *breathin'!*" The younger man raised his fists.

It promised to be a bloody fight when a hunting dog was insulted. Jake rolled his eyes in disgust. Before the first blows could be exchanged, he was standing between the antagonists. Both squirmed with frustrated fury, while the other customers looked on. All three dogs in the place were staring, their ears laid back.

"There'll be no fights in the Prairie Chicken," Jake said. "Kill each other outside—nobody cares."

The man whose dog had been insulted wanted revenge. "I'll kill him here and now!" he snarled with bared teeth. "Before the coward has a chance to run."

Jake stared coldly into the man's eyes. "Didn't you hear what I said? Maybe you'd like to take me on, instead."

These words hit the brawler like a fist in the face. His body sagged and he stepped back. "I want no trouble with you, Sheriff."

Jake turned to the second man. "What about you?"

"I didn't start nothin'," he wheezed.

"Than take it on out." Jake turned his back and strode calmly to the bar. Three days of rain had people on edge. Usually trouble didn't begin this early in the evening.

Russell had ordered them each another beer. "Good thing you were here." He pushed a fresh mug in front of his cousin. "I was about to ask if you'd look over my orders and see if you can find some ways to cut costs on that damn pool."

"If you're looking for inferior materials, forget it. There's no legal way. You undercut the Eversville bid because you wanted the job. Now you've got it. Don't involve me, Russ."

He swallowed half the beer. MacGuire Construction had been founded by their fathers. Six years ago Russell had bought Jake's share in the company when Jake was in a financial bind. He refused to allow Jake to borrow with the firm as collateral. Now, finishing the municipal pool was Russell's problem. Especially after taking it upon himself to have that expensive Brutus statue made.

But the problem of collecting some forty years of municipal and county taxes on Maude O'Connor's property—that was Jake's problem. He would have to put the house and the land on the auction block, no doubt. First thing tomorrow, he'd look up the name and address of the O'Connor heir and send the poor devil a bill. The townspeople were impatiently waiting for the pool they had been promised by midsummer.

"I assumed you were smarter than you are," he complained to Russell. "You knew there wasn't enough money when you tendered the bid. You don't seriously believe anybody is going to pay those taxes, do you? All we'll have is a worthless, battered old house."

"It sits on twenty acres of good land."

Jake shrugged. Admittedly, the land adjoining the river was prime. He often fished on that stretch of shore, under the biggest cottonwood trees he'd ever seen.

Hell, he thought. If it weren't for those outstanding taxes, he might buy that land himself. But the house—no one would buy that damned thing. Not even Nellie Jean Schrock, who made a habit of accumulating as much of Devil's Fork real estate as she could, just as her father had done. He glanced over at Nellie Jean, whose eyes were glazed over with love while she watched Preacher Whitney strum his polished guitar. The unsinkable Miss Schrock, who ran the mayor's office with such efficiency—even she could become a fool for love.

People who loved so blindly were all fools, he thought. Love never brought anything but heartache, the kind of heartache the preacher was crooning about this very moment. Suddenly Jake couldn't stand listening to the song a moment longer, nor the laughter in the saloon, nor Russell at his elbow talking business.

The taste of rain promised to be better than the taste of beer, the wail of the wind better than the music or the drone of human voices. Jake straightened and pushed away from the bar.

"See you tomorrow," he said.

Russell scowled. "You're leaving? You just got here."

"Things to do."

As he always did, he gave the preacher a thumbs-up on his way out, his way of offering his appreciation for the music. Donald nodded, smiled and kept singing.

Outside, Jake stood in the relentless cool rain thinking about the flowers he had placed on the summer grass, now drenched and pounded and pathetic. Loneliness was a part of his life because, caught in the pain of the past, he refused to trust any woman again. And how much of his loneliness, he'd begun to ask himself lately, was the fault of his own male ego? Somewhere in the community of Devil's Fork was a man who'd been his wife's lover. That man was walking the streets, still laughing behind his back, and until he knew who it was, Jake couldn't be free enough of the past to focus on the future.

2

ON AN AFTERNOON in early June, Dana French sat in her Dallas studio sorting proofs. An old chum from high school, visiting from St. Louis, was pacing back and forth in front of photographs displayed on the walls.

The photos were all in black and white: a tanned telephone lineman on his pole, muscles bulging in a tank top; a construction worker in a hard hat and no shirt, the top snap of his jeans undone; a handsome executive rushing for a taxi, his hair blowing in the wind and his coat flying open; a smiling police officer in short sleeves and tight pants; and a scantily clad tennis pro bending to return a fast serve.

"Where do you *find* these hunks?"

Dana looked up from her desk, dark eyes sparkling. "I have an eye for masculine beauty."

"Whew, I guess!" Barbara's short red hair gleamed in the sunlight coming in through the studio window. "How do you recruit? Do you scout the streets and byways and then just walk up to these guys and ask them to pose for you?"

"It amounts to that. I show them the calendars I've done and ask if they're interested. I've never met one yet who wasn't. Hunks have monstrous egos."

Barbara sat on the edge of the desk and glanced over the photos her old schoolmate was sorting—men in various stages of undress. "Dana, you have the most enviable profession in the civilized world."

Dana smiled. "My calendar business is doing even better than I anticipated. After just two years it's bringing in more money than all my other photography work put together. I admit I love it." She brushed her smooth, honey-blond hair back from her neck and continued to sort the proofs into three piles. So much had happened since her high school days with Barbara, most of which she did not wish to share. Like her two engagements—better forgotten. John had objected to her profession from the moment they became engaged. His jealousy of her models had him trying to convince her she would never make it working for herself. He had given her an ultimatum. She had chosen her work and her freedom and never regretted it. Walt had been the opposite; he had seen her potential and had wanted to make himself a part of it. Dana had not wanted someone riding on her shoulders, and had broken off that engagement, too. It just wasn't worth it, trying to find the right man to share her life with. Since Walt, it had been easier alone.

Barbara lit a cigarette and blew out a cloud of smoke slowly. "Do you date any of these gorgeous specimens?"

"Nope. Never mix business with pleasure."

"That's the silliest thing I ever heard. Your business *is* pleasure."

Dana shrugged. "Maybe their egos get in the way, Barb, I don't know. I've never met one who really interested me."

"Some free-spirited single lady *you* are!" Barbara picked up a proof of a lifeguard on a beach and studied it with a sigh. "If you ask me, all this concentration on male anatomy has jaded you on men. Oh, would that I suffered such an affliction! I can't take looking at all these shiny male bodies so early in the day and on an empty stomach. Isn't there someplace around here we can go have a fattening brunch?"

Dana looked at her watch. It was impossible to work with Barbara visiting, but it had been fun getting together after eight years. Tomorrow Barb was continuing on to California, so the work could wait until then. "I know a good place," she said.

"Good. Maybe it has a sweating hunk cook you can photograph scrambling eggs and frying mean beans."

The postman walked in as Dana was finishing the sorting. He greeted her with a smile and a small stack of mail. "Registered letter here for Dana French."

"Thanks." She signed hurriedly and inspected the letter. "This looks official, Barb. It's from the tax assessor's office in Devil's Fork, Colorado."

"Devil's Fork? What town would have a pun for a name?"

"The weirdest town I've ever been in. I was there once when I was fourteen to visit my eccentric great-aunt Maude, and from what I remember, her friends were as strange, too."

Dana felt a stab of fear. She hadn't heard from her great-aunt in nearly a year. Now there was this letter from a county office. Her heart sank. *Oh, damn,* she thought.

Barbara waited while she read the letter. "What is it?"

"What I feared. My great-aunt passed away last week. I feel guilty for not having kept in better touch with her. She was such an odd old character, but sweet, really nice to me when I visited her the summer my mother died. Poor Aunt Maude. I wish I'd known about this before her funeral."

"Would you have gone?"

"Yeah, maybe. Oh, it's awful to think of traveling to her funeral when I should have gone to see her when she was alive, instead. Hell." Dana's attention returned to the letter in her hand.

Barbara cocked her head. "Did she leave you something?"

Dana nodded slowly. "She left me everything she had, her house and everything in it. She had no one else, no children of her own." She squinted at the paper, frowning. "Ye gods, Barb, according to this, Maude owed twenty-nine thousand, seven hundred sixty-six dollars and eighteen cents in back taxes—which the city is demanding from *me!*"

"That's almost thirty thousand dollars! How could she owe thirty thousand dollars in taxes?"

"Obviously by not paying. She must not have paid taxes on that house for forty or fifty years!"

"Whoa. Is it a fabulous house?"

"It's a big frame house on the edge of town. Built around 1915. I remember a shady lane leading up to it and a wide porch. It's stuffed full of antiques." She slapped the paper. "The city assessor is demanding payment or they will take the house!"

She slumped in her chair, trying to assimilate this unwelcome intrusion in her life. "I'll have to sell Maude's house. I wonder how the real-estate market is in Devil's Fork. I can't imagine anyone wanting to live there."

Barbara slid off the desk and straightened her skirt. "Looks like you're headed for Satan's Fork whether you like it or not."

The letter requested that she contact the assessor's office, where the deed and the keys to the house were being held for her. Surely it was worth more than thirty thousand dollars! And the contents? They were hers, too. Dana remembered claw-footed chairs and tables, needlepoint seats and a gold-edged mirror, and pieces of china and silver.

Barb was right. There was no choice but to go to Devil's Fork. She couldn't just let the city take the house. She would inventory Maude's possessions, see what could be sold and what she wanted to keep.

Throughout brunch, Dana's mind was in Devil's Fork. She would have to close up shop for a week or two and cancel her shoots. She felt a headache coming on, and why not? She had just inherited a thirty thousand-dollar debt.

Barbara read her mind. "Do you have pressing business you'll have to cancel?"

"Several appointments, including two portfolio shoots for male models, and a shoot at a mall fashion show."

"Sounds like your professional reputation is spreading."

"Yeah." Dana smiled. "I'm considered an expert at photographing male bodies. Who'd have thought when we took that amateur photo class in high school that it would someday come to this?"

"I know you had to struggle for a while."

"When I was working for somebody else after college, yes. Until I decided to do my own thing."

"How *did* you decide to do calendars? The last I heard you were engaged to marry a lawyer. John something. What happened?"

"I began selling photographs of men to a gallery and then decided there was money in 'hunk' calendars. John took one look at my first few sets of proofs and decided no wife of his was going to do such work. He didn't understand photographic art, and I didn't understand why a wife needed permission for her own career. So we went our separate ways."

Even then, after John and before Walt, there had been lean years. But a year and a half ago Dana had used her savings to put a down payment on a newly zoned-for-business house in a Dallas suburb. She'd converted the downstairs to a studio and moved into the cozy second story and told Walt goodbye. She was not getting rich yet, but she was doing well. Walt had slunk off in search of another woman with a promising career.

Barbara finished her ham-and-cheese omelet. "If I didn't have this job waiting for me in San Diego, I'd go with you. I've always wanted to visit Colorado. Is this Satan's Fork in the mountains by any chance?"

"The Rocky Mountain peaks are visible from the town. Peaks with snow all summer long. Devil's Fork sits in a deep valley. I don't remember much about that summer, except for Maude's house and the women's club meetings she held there—ladies in hats at the dining table eating cake and pie and telling tales about everybody in town. I loved sitting on the stairs and listening to all the gossip." She paused. "I hate the thought of going back and finding Maude's house empty."

IT WAS A LONG DRIVE from Texas, and Dana had time to examine her memories of Devil's Fork. The approach was as she remembered, the river bridge crossing just beyond the little airport and the huge enormous trees that lined the streets familiar. But the town center—a square of three blocks, with buildings wearing faces more than half a century old—looked different.

That statue had not been there before. A huge figure of a German shepherd dominated the square. Beside him stood a man in pioneer dress, leaning down to rest a hand on the dog's regal head. An impressive work of art for such a small community. Below the figures in big letters were the words "Brutus—Founding Hero." The man or the dog? she wondered.

It was just after ten in the morning when Dana pulled into the parking lot of the municipal building. She felt a sense of dread as she strode up the walkway to the front steps.

The building had the musty dusty atmosphere of a place unchanged for decades. The corridor smelled of stale cigar smoke. No directory was needed; there were only a few doors, and on the glass of one, the words "Tax Office."

The office's only occupant was a woman in her early thirties—Betsy Ostergren, according to the nameplate on her desk. Ms. Ostergren, who was reading a *Motorcycle Escapades* magazine, didn't look up until Dana was standing in front of her desk.

Dana pulled the letter from her shoulder bag and handed it to the receptionist. "I'm Dana French."

Betsy glanced at the letter. "Oh yes!" She studied Dana while she opened the top drawer of the desk. "I have your file right here."

I'm top priority, Dana thought. *Right in front,* And why not? The city wanted its twenty-nine thousand, seven hundred sixty-six dollars and eighteen cents. Why they hadn't managed to collect it from Maude was a mystery. Or maybe not, knowing Maude, who had once remarked that she—unlike everybody else—did not believe in either death or taxes.

Betsy Ostergren placed a manila folder on the desk and said formally, "I have the deed to the O'Connor house and also the keys. Have you some identification, please?"

Dana produced her driver's license. The woman gazed at it, then looked up and smiled. "I knew Mrs. O'Connor. She taught my mother in third grade. Every one of her classes planted a tree in the park as a class project. Now that section is called O'Connor Grove."

Dana smiled. "I'd forgotten she taught school years ago."

"Oh, my, yes. Mrs. O'Connor allowed kids to bring their dogs to school. Any dog that behaved was allowed to stay. She said it was important for dogs to learn to be responsible citizens."

Dana wished she had known her great-aunt better. "The school board went along with this?"

"Heavens, yes. The Ladies' Club backed her on the issue and the board didn't dare start trouble with them. Anyway, no one would have objected. People in this town are especially fond of dogs."

Dana returned her driver's license to her wallet. "I like a place where dogs are popular and women have clout."

"Oh, women don't have the same clout anymore, I'm afraid. The members of the wonderful Ladies' Club have all passed away."

"And a shame it is, too!" said a voice from behind them. The tall woman approaching was wearing a gray-and-white-striped seersucker suit with a gray blouse. She was in her mid-thirties and wore no make-up except for bright pink lipstick. Her face was not pretty, but her eyes were intelligent and friendly.

"This is Nellie Jean Schrock," Betsy said. "Nellie Jean works in the mayor's office. And *this*, Nellie Jean, is Maude O'Connor's niece, Dana French."

Nellie Jean shook Dana's hand, then said, "Your aunt was the last of a great breed, Dana. She didn't let anyone interfere with her principles, including her belief that paying taxes was unAmerican. She said that issue should have been settled when we broke away from England. Mayor MacGuire didn't dare do anything about it, either, not if he wanted to stay in office." She sighed. "She was the last of the ladies of spunk. Now the town is dominated by hardheaded males—my boss, the mayor, and Betsy's boss, the sheriff."

"But that's only two men," Dana said.

"Right. The MacGuire cousins. They control everything, and people are convinced they're the best thing that ever happened to Devil's Fork. I openly disagree. I cause all the unrest I can around here, but the mayor keeps me on because I know more about running his office than he does."

Dana looked at the letter in her hand. "The tax assessor is also a MacGuire."

"That's Jake. The sheriff. He holds two jobs, so they can better control the city. The tax job isn't full-time, never has been, and nobody wants it. Jake took it on as a favor to his cousin. Betsy here, she runs this tax office. Jake couldn't get along without her. He's too busy sheriffing, walking around with his gun on his hip, daring anybody to get one inch out of line."

"The Lone Ranger," Betsy grinned. "People are scared to death of him. But he keeps law and order, you have to give him that."

"Great," Dana said, discouraged. "This is the guy I have to deal with about Maude's tax debt. Where is he?"

"He only comes in to the office here once or twice a week. Works by appointment. He'll call you and set up a time." She pushed some papers across the desk. "If you'll just sign these before you take possession of the house..."

"What are you going to do with the old house?" Nellie Jean asked.

"Sell it to pay the taxes."

The two women exchanged glances.

Betsy said, "After you phoned you were coming I checked on the utilities. All the bills are paid up until the end of the month, so you won't be in the dark out there. If there's anything I can do to help, let me know." She handed Dana the keys. "Just a word of warning. When you get an appointment with Jake MacGuire, make sure you're on time. My boss isn't good about being kept waiting."

THE HOUSE, located on the edge of town near the river, was as large as Dana remembered. It was a white frame, two-story building with a wide front porch. At fourteen, Dana had swung on the porch swing sniffing the fragrance of honeysuckle and listening to the croaking of frogs on the riverbank.

She entered the house now longing for her great-aunt's welcoming voice and one of her crushing hugs. The scent of Maude's lavender perfume still hung on the air . A kaleidoscope of memories filled Dana's mind— Maude's rose crepe dress with silver beads on the front, the lacy nightgown she wore down to breakfast, orange-pekoe tea and vanilla cookies on the front porch with a view of green farmland and the trees along the river, the bookshelf in the den her great-aunt had always dusted with the long-handled ostrich-feather duster.

How eerily silent the house was. It seemed alive and dead at the same time. Dana didn't feel like an intruder, though. Maude wanted her to be there. Wandering through the house, absorbed in the personality and comfort of it, she began to feel that she was not alone. As though she were being watched.

It's only my memories following me, she thought as she circled through the downstairs rooms. The sunny kitchen was welcoming, with its glass-door cupboards and the checkered tablecloth and Maude's collection of salt-and-pepper souvenirs.

All this was hers! It only now hit her fully that this house belonged to her. Aunt Maude's possessions were loved and well cared for, and it was going to break her heart to sell them. The thought of getting rid of the beautiful furnishings felt like a betrayal to Aunt Maude and the house.

Upstairs was a wide carpeted hallway lined with a collection of photographs. At the end stood a bureau with a mirror that reflected the pink walls. Four bedrooms and a bath opened off the hall. She crossed to Maude's bedroom.

The chintz curtains were drawn, the bed carefully made. Someone had been here since the funeral to take care of the house; everything was freshly dusted. In one corner of the spacious bedroom was an antique rolltop writing desk where Aunt Maude had written letters before her afternoon nap. Inside it were the dozen pigeonholes and mysterious tiny drawers that had fascinated Dana as a girl.

Dana opened the miniature drawers one by one as she had years ago. In one of them was a pair of antique eyeglasses in ornate frames, unlike any Dana had ever seen.

"What a collector wouldn't give for these!" she said aloud, slipping on the glasses. The lenses did not magnify the objects in the room; everything looked the same except for a slight rose tint.

A movement across the room caught her eye. Turning, she drew a startled breath. An old woman was sitting in the rocking chair! She was wearing a dress of forest-green silk and silk stockings and lace-up shoes. Her hair was white and cut very short around her face, and she was smiling.

Dana yanked off the glasses, and the old lady disappeared.

Her heart pounded like a drum. Without the glasses, the rocking chair was empty. But it was rocking.

What had she seen?

A ghost?

3

DANA BACKED to the bed and sank onto it, trembling with fright. The figure she had seen was not Aunt Maude. Who was it? *What* was it?

Her impulse was to throw the cursed glasses down and run from the room, but as she sat frozen on the bed she realized she had no place to run. This was her house. If there was something . . . a ghost . . . here, she was going to have to deal with it. Anyway, it must have been her imagination. Or she had fallen asleep and was dreaming.

Hesitantly she donned the glasses again. The old woman was there, still smiling.

"Don't be alarmed," she said in a sweet voice. "It's just me . . . Louise."

Dana struggled for her voice and finally was able to ask, "Why can I only see you with these glasses?"

"It is magical, isn't? We were so afraid you might not try them on."

With her heart pounding so loudly the beat seemed deafening, Dana was surprised at how clearly she could hear the woman's faint voice. "We?" she squeaked.

"My friends and I, and your lovely aunt." The old woman looked about. "Now, where is that scamp Maude? Not here to greet you?"

A second later Maude O'Connor appeared in the doorway looking exactly as Dana remembered her. She was dressed in a loose-fitting mauve dress with linen embroidery on the bodice, bone-colored shoes with thick heels, and a string of pearls. Her gray hair was knotted in a bun in back, a few loose wisps framed her face. She was smiling prettily, the smile Dana remembered so well.

"Of course I'm here, Louise," she said in the familiar gravelly voice. "Dana, my dear, welcome! How fortunate you found the glasses so quickly, but then I knew you'd look in my writing desk. You loved the desk so. My goodness, you've gone utterly *white*, my dear. Are you all right?"

Dana blinked. "No, I'm not all right! I thought . . ." The words sounded extremely foolish as they came out of her mouth. "I thought you were dead."

"Of course I'm dead. Well, by your standards, at least. But as I always told you, there is really no such thing as death. As you can see, I'm still here." She turned and gestured. "You've met Louise."

"Yes . . ." Dana fumbled with the glasses, pushed them down on her nose and peered over the top. The doorway was empty. But when she looked through the rose-tinted glasses again, her aunt stood there looking as alive as ever.

Well, not quite. There was an odd echo in her voice, and her arms and legs moved in a kind of slow motion when she stepped out of the doorway and into the room. Maude sat on the satin chair in front of her dressing table where once she had brushed her hair and told Dana stories. "You look speechless, my dear. What is wrong? Don't you believe in ghosts?"

"I don't—didn't think so . . ."

"But I distinctly remember telling you ghosts are very real. At the time you visited me—let me think—that would have been about twelve years ago…yes. At that time Evelyn's spirit was here and so was Rosella's."

Dana's fear began to drain away. What was there to be afraid of, after all? Aunt Maude was no different, really. Her spirit had not left her home, that was all. Her voice was so calming, so reassuring, like that of an adult showing a child something of the world for the first time. No, there was nothing to be afraid of, but there was the mystery to marvel at—Aunt Maude was still here! How wonderful!

"Don't you remember my telling you this house was haunted and how glorious it was?" her aunt asked.

"I thought you were just making it up, that it was a game." Dana's voice was stronger now. Somehow it was beginning to seem natural talking with her great-aunt again, here in her pink and white bedroom. "Why have you stayed in your house?" she asked Maude.

"Where else would I be? This is where I belong—in this house with all its memories. You still look very pale, dear. Why don't you make yourself a cup of tea? Remember the orange-pekoe tea you loved? There's some in the kitchen."

"That's not a bad idea," Dana said, rising slowly from the bed. Her legs were shaking as she made her way out of the room and down the stairs, carrying the glasses. She wondered if she would have the courage to wear them if every time she put them on she saw a ghost.

The tea bags were in the cookie jar, where they'd always been. While the tea steeped, she put on the eye-glasses again and nervously glanced behind her.

She jumped and nearly spilled the tea. A third old lady—a pudgy one—was in the kitchen with her.

"I didn't mean to startle you," the ghost said in her silvery echo-voice. "My name is Rosella. I was here when you visited before, but you didn't see me then. My, you've grown into a lovely young woman, haven't you?"

Disbelief thinned Dana's voice. "You were here then?"

"Ah, yes. But your aunt couldn't tell you about the magical glasses because you were too young, and you would have repeated the story and people wouldn't have believed you."

Before she could respond, Dana spied another face peering from the back hallway—another old lady, looking in curiously. They seemed to be everywhere! She was surrounded!

This one wore a hat covered with silk flowers. "Hello," the ghost said shyly, moving into the room. "At last I am to meet Maude's niece! My name is Frances."

How many ghosts were there?

Before Dana could respond to Frances, her aunt appeared. "We're gathering in the living room, Dana dear. Frances, Rosella, meeting time!"

I'm dreaming this, Dana thought as she picked up her teacup with unsteady hands, and joined her deceased aunt and friends.

She stood in the archway wearing the antique spectacles and holding the cup of tea, and looked at a room full of ghosts. There were six of them, seated in chairs and on the sofa, wearing crepes and satins and silk knits.

A tall thin figure rose from her chair and took a step forward. Dana recognized the pinkish dyed hair and piercing blue eyes and nose like a little bird's beak. This was a friend of Maude's whom she had met twelve years ago, but she couldn't remember her name.

"We have been waiting for you, now that the house is yours." The ghost smiled. "My name is Evelyn. Do you remember me? I'd like to present to you—" her hand swept over the group slowly as she recited their names "—Rosella, Louise, Inez, Frances and, of course, your beloved Maude. We are the Ladies' Club of Devil's Fork."

The Ladies' Club? Dana thought. *Good Lord!*

She sat down on the one remaining chair, set her cup on the table and stared at them. Six old ladies gazed at her in anticipation. She was smack in the center of a Ladies' Club meeting—the notorious Ladies' Club! It was just too bizarre.

The ghost named Inez spoke. "I'm afraid we come with the house, dear. Maude assured us this would be fine. We are no bother, truly. You cannot even see us without the glasses, and you can hear us only when you can see us."

"Why is that?" Dana asked. "Why do these glasses make it possible for me to see and hear you?"

Her great-aunt answered. "We haven't the faintest idea. The glasses belonged to Louise originally—a family heirloom. Just before Louise crossed over, she gave the glasses to me and told me to keep them safe and put them on sometimes and think of her. When I kept this promise, we discovered I could see and talk to her. We don't know why. We don't even know where the glasses came from, except that they're very old."

"We only know that they're magical," Louise said. "I was the first to cross into the spirit world and I didn't want to leave my friends—our club—and so I didn't leave. I stayed and attended every meeting here in this house, just as before." She chuckled. "I missed a meeting because of my funeral, but I was not about to miss any more."

"And I followed," Rosella said. "I stayed, too, and we kept our little group intact. Some of us were spirit and some were earthbound, but it didn't matter. We just carried on as always. Now we're all here in spirit, but nothing is changed, except we have more time to spend together."

Evelyn, the ghost with pink hair, spoke up. "No, now that Maude has joined us, it's not the same, because we have no spokesperson on the other side! It's difficult without someone who can mingle among the living."

The little flowers on Frances's hat bobbed back and forth as she shook her head in frustration. "We are *stuck* in here! How are we to find *out* what is going *on?*"

Rosella spoke from her place on the sofa. "Perhaps you would be the spokesperson for our club, Dana dear! We do need a spokesperson who's still . . . as you say . . . alive."

"But I don't live here," Dana protested, hearing the echo of her own voice, knowing hers was the only voice any living person could hear. "I live in Dallas, and I can't be away from my business for too long. I only came to . . ."

Her voice trailed away as a wave of reality hit, making her feel ill. She had come to *sell* the house! She looked at the ghosts who lived here and could not say it.

The ladies of the club exchanged grave glances. "We know, of course, that your home is in Texas," Aunt Maude said. "We shan't discuss it now. It's going to take you some time to get used to us—we understand that. After all, you didn't know we were here. No one knows."

"Ah, but there are rumors in the town," Frances said, her voice crackling with mischief. "Rumors about ghosts in this house. Ghosts? Here? In Maude's lovely home?"

"*Imagine* people saying the house is haunted!" Inez giggled. "Such a vicious rumor!"

Dana reached for her tea, needing something warm and soothing in her queasy stomach. She jumped, startled, when the telephone rang.

"The phone is in the kitchen," Maude said. "In case you decide to answer it."

"Yes," Dana said numbly. "All right." She slipped the eyeglasses into her shirt pocket, went to the kitchen and picked up the phone on the fifth ring.

"Is this Dana French?" The masculine voice was deep and sexy enough to alert her.

"Yes."

"This is Jake MacGuire. My secretary informed me you've arrived in Devil's Fork. My condolences on the loss of your aunt."

"Thank you," Dana muttered. The condolence sounded more obligatory than sincere.

He continued brusquely, "We have a tax bill to discuss. I'd like to come out there this afternoon at five o'clock."

"Out here?"

"I'm not in my office this afternoon, but I'll finish up at the courthouse by five. I'll stop on my way home."

Dana swallowed, remembering what Betsy Oster-gren had told her about this man. She had better not try to negotiate another time. Well, at least she didn't have to go back into town. Perhaps his getting to the tax business as soon as possible showed he was being considerate. Or perhaps he was being pushy. Or maybe he wanted to have a look at the interior of the house to assess the value of Maude's possessions.

Whatever the reason, he was certainly abrupt. From what she had heard about Jake MacGuire, Dana was afraid she was facing an ordeal.

"I'll expect you about five, then," she said flatly.

The clock on the kitchen wall said one thirty-six. Dana felt drained of energy. Emotional overload was sapping her strength. She had no desire to go back into the living room and try to make conversation with a bunch of chattering ghosts. She was going to have to tell this MacGuire that she had no money for the taxes. Her only option was to discuss the sale of the house with him. The Ladies' Club wouldn't like that at all!

"Damn," she muttered.

The blue-and-white flowered curtain began flapping, even though the window was not open. Feeling a presence, Dana slipped the glasses on. Maude and Rosella and Evelyn were standing beside the kitchen table.

"Was that Sheriff MacGuire on the phone?" Maude asked.

She nodded. "He's coming to talk about collecting your taxes from me, Aunt Maude. How did you manage to accumulate almost thirty thousand dollars in unpaid taxes? Did you never pay property tax?"

"Certainly not. We Americans are supposed to be free from taxes. That's what the War of Independence was all about. They'll not take my money to buy weapons to blow people up. This is my property. I don't have to pay to be here."

"How did you get away with it, though? With a tax assessor like this Jake MacGuire?"

Rosella grinned. "The town couldn't take any forcible action to collect because Maude is too well liked, and when the bill got so outrageously high... Well, who has that much money stashed away? If the mayor had pressed the issue, he would have been nudged right out of office, and he knew it."

"They intend to collect now." Dana sighed. "And I don't have that kind of money. My savings went for my studio—which is also where I live. All I have to my credit are debts."

"Oh, this is terrible," Evelyn said, shaking her gray locks. "Those brats! I always said Jake and Russell were awful brats. Always creating mischief when they were kids—getting into fights, stirring up trouble. I don't know how Inez managed to put up with them."

"Inez is their grandmother," Rosella explained to Dana. "Jake's and the mayor's. Their fathers were brothers."

Inez appeared in the doorway. She was a small pretty woman with few wrinkles and salt-and-pepper hair worn in a loose bun. She wore a fine silk dress of slate blue with lace collar and cuffs. "It's true that those boys were always getting into trouble," she said, walking into the room. "I always thought Russell was meaner, but he would try to cover his trail and put on an angel face and blame someone else—usually Jake—for his misdemeanors. Russell is older, but he was always a little afraid of Jake."

"Everybody is afraid of Jake," Evelyn said.

Inez sighed. "I suppose so, yet he was a sweet child who used to bring me bouquets of wildflowers that he picked in the fields." Another sigh. "I wonder where that sweetness has gone."

Rosella, although she looked very stout, raised herself easily onto the kitchen counter and sat dangling her plump legs over the edge. "Certainly none of that sweetness shows in your grandson these days. Dana, dear, you must be careful not to rub this man the wrong way. He can be most unpleasant. Don't let him intimidate you. He will if he can. He intimidates everybody."

Dana was grateful for the warnings and glad she did not have to face the man alone, even though he wouldn't know they weren't alone. Surely he would be reasonable about giving her time to try to sell the house. Surely he wouldn't just *take* it, even though legally he could.

"I'm not looking forward to meeting your sheriff," she said. "He isn't actually *mean*, is he?"

"Mean as they come," Maude said. "Since he became sheriff, there hasn't been much crime in Devil's Fork."

His grandmother shook her head sadly. "I can't think of Jake as mean. As a child he protected the little girls from bullies. From snakes and spiders, too. And when I read him bedtime stories, he always asked for *Mike of Thunder Mountain*, about a boy of the West and his horse Lightfoot. They rescued a damsel in every episode."

Her eyes closed as she remembered days long past. "I took care of him when he was sick. I mended his teddy bear when the eyes fell off and the feet and hands wore through to the stuffing. We took out my basket of fabric scraps so Jake could pick what he wanted for Harley's—that was the bear's name—hands and feet. He choose black polka dots. I wonder whatever became of that bear."

Dana laughed. "If he likes polka dots, I ought to wear my black-and-white polka-dot dress and hope that subconsciously he'll associate it with his teddy bear and it'll put him in an agreeable mood."

Inez chuckled. "He always loved dots. If you want him in a good mood to confront this awful tax business, wear dots and serve him blueberryderries. He won't be so intimidating, then. He'll be purring like a puppy when its tummy is scratched."

"Puppies don't purr," Rosella said, disgusted.

"But wait! What a marvelous idea this is!" Maude shrieked. "To soften up the tax collector! The noble start of a workable scheme to save our house!" She turned to Inez. "What on earth are blueberryderries?"

"My special pastries. My secret recipe. Oh, how Jake and Russell would beg for those when they were lads! Well, even when they were grown! I will give you my recipe, Dana, and we'll make up a perfect batch. Jake would turn somersaults and bay at the moon for a taste of my blueberryderries."

"This sounds fun!" Dana exclaimed.

"Oh, *what* fun! And you will serve them with cinnamon milk, which Jake used to love. He won't be throwing his weight around with blueberryderries and cinnamon milk in his tummy, I guarantee."

Dana glanced at the clock. "I'd better go shopping for the ingredients. There's no time to waste."

Louise, who had been listening from the doorway, said excitedly, "The roadside grocery on the corner as you reach town will have everything you need." From her perch on the countertop, Rosella leaned toward Dana with a confidence to share. "The man who runs that grocery had an affair with his wife's best friend, and they got caught when their rowboat drifted into a cove where the Carson twins were having a picnic."

"Never mind that now," Inez said. "We have our own plot brewing here. Dana, there is a pencil and paper in the top drawer. I will tell you what to buy."

BY FOUR O'CLOCK the blueberryderries were in the oven and the plot was well in hand. The Ladies' Club members were wild with excitement. This was like the wonderful conspiracies of the old days now that they were engaged in a battle to save their home from the determined officials of Devil's Fork. Dana was as giddy as the rest of them. She was nervously dropping things as she straightened the kitchen and washed the cooking utensils.

"I need to know the parameters for mellowing this guy," Dana said, caught up in the intrigue. "If he's married..."

"His wife died several years ago," Frances said softly.

"So you see, he's not married," Inez agreed—too quickly. The subject seemed to make the ghosts uncomfortable.

"He is single," Rosella chimed in. "So no need to hold back—give him as many blueberryderries as he wants. If his stomach rebels, so much the better. It might make him forget what he came for."

"Oh my, they *are* beastly rich," Inez said. "If he turns green, give him a cinnamon stick to suck on. I used to do that."

Maude was pacing nervously. "Dana, don't be alarmed and intimidated when you see that he's armed. Jake carries a gun."

"And a slingshot," Frances added. "He walks around with a slingshot sticking out of his back pocket."

"Surely your sheriff doesn't shoot people with a slingshot!" Dana exclaimed as she dried the mixing bowl.

"Not people," Inez said. "He uses it to get livestock off the roads. Nevertheless, if he does have the thing, it would be unwise to bring up the subject of slingshots. It might remind him of the time he made a complete fool of himself trying to be a human slingshot."

Inez chuckled, then began to laugh. The room fell silent as the other ghosts and Dana waited eagerly for the tale, although Dana was the only one who'd never heard it.

Inez giggled. "He was just a boy and up to boyish pranks. Down at the tennis courts, he decided if his friends pulled back on the net with all their strength, it would become a slingshot, and he could position himself in the center and shoot himself through the air like a rocket. So eight or ten kids pulled on the net until it was bent with tension. When they all released at once, Jake went bouncing over the court like a wound-up ballerina. He couldn't stop the momentum before he had broken every toe on both feet. He stubbornly rode his bike home in agony and humiliation. As long as any of the witnesses are alive, he will never live it down. So don't mention slingshots."

The mental picture was so absurd Dana hoped she wouldn't think of it when he was present. But of course she knew she would, and she'd have to struggle not to laugh.

The oven timer buzzed. The blueberryderries were done. Inez said, "Check to see if they're golden brown on the edges!"

The aroma of the freshly baked pastries filled the house. "Heavenly!" Dana breathed as she set the pan on a cooling rack, then wiped her hands on the seat of her jeans. "It's getting late! I'd better hurry and unpack my polka-dot dress."

Despite her armor—blueberryderries and polka dots—she couldn't suppress her dread at meeting this grouchy gun-toting widower.

4

A CALL CAME as Jake was about to leave his office.

"Sheriff, this is Bradford Jones out on Route Two. I'm calling to report some kids in a red car speeding and running cars off the road. The kids are drinking and yelling obscenities. They ran a car into a five-foot ditch."

Jake's jaw muscles tightened. "A red sports car?"

"Yeah," Jones answered. "It ain't from Devil's Fork."

"Those kids are from Eversville. I've had problems with them before. Where did you see the car?"

"By my place. Hope you come before they kill somebody."

It was a quarter to five. Jake hoped this wouldn't make him too late for his appointment with Dana French. The red sports car belonged to the son of an Eversville town official who made a habit of bailing his kid out of trouble. The boy had been ticketed twice, and the father had paid two hefty traffic fines.

Ten minutes later Jake spotted the car on the county road, weaving erratically. When he turned on his police siren the car sped up. Jake pressed the accelerator and gave chase, finally maneuvering the car onto the shoulder where its wheels spun in the mud. The four boys in the car were drinking cans of beer and laughing insolently as the law officer approached.

"Whatsa matter, Sheriff?" the driver sneered. "You got a problem?"

"Nope," Jake answered, approaching the window. "You have."

The boy wiped his nose with his sleeve and sniffed. "We didn't do nothin'. Just out for a little ride."

"You've been warned twice," Jake growled. "Which is one time more than I warn anybody else." When he'd stopped the same four boys on two previous occasions, they had been driving recklessly, but there had been no evidence of drinking. This time they were so inebriated it was a wonder the high-speed car stayed on the road.

One of the boys rolled down the back window and squinted up at Jake, grinning challengingly. "You ain't gonna arrest us, are you? And make us go to Brian's old man for bail money? He wouldn't like to hear about more trouble from the law down here."

"Nope. I'm not gonna arrest you."

"That's more like it, be a good sheriff," the driver, Brian Arnold, said smiling.

Jake returned the smile, but it did not reach his hard, steel-colored eyes. He stepped back and whipped his pistol from its holster. Four shots rang out.

One for each tire.

He turned without another word, got into his pickup, turned off the blinking lights and started the engine, ignoring the drunken yells of the four teenagers. They were a good twenty miles from Eversville, which was over the county line. How they got home was their problem. At least they weren't likely to kill themselves or someone else in the process.

IN THE BIG WHITE HOUSE by the river, Dana was beginning to pace. The tax assessor, who insisted that people be prompt, was late. Already fifteen minutes late.

When the doorbell finally rang, she set the magical eyeglasses on a shelf in the kitchen, smoothed the skirt of her polka-dot dress, then drew a deep breath as she walked to the door and swung it open.

Inez MacGuire's grandson stood more than six feet tall with shoulders as wide as a mountain and eyes as blue as the sky. Dana, the photographer, the connoisseur of manhood, expert on male beauty, nearly choked.

Late-afternoon sunlight silvered the badge on his short-sleeved khaki shirt. A gun-belt was strapped over the top of his tight jeans. He wore no hat; his dark hair, waved by a breeze, curled over his forehead.

"Dana French?" The resonant voice made her think of a radio deejay in Dallas.

"Yes," she said, smiling. "Come in, Sheriff."

The dots, she decided, were distracting him, because he looked at her in a bewildered way. She led him through the hall, and caught a reflection of bouncing polka dots as she passed by the mirror.

"This shouldn't take long," the deep voice uttered, then added, as if from far away, "That smell . . ."

She turned. "Night of an Orange Moon. Do you like it?"

"What?" He was breathing deeply.

"My perfume."

"Not perfume. Something baking . . ."

"Oh, that. I've just whipped up some little pastries. Will you have some? Of course you will. Just off work, you must be hungry. Was it a busy day?"

"I'm late because I was on a call," he said distractedly at the entrance to the kitchen.

She bustled ahead and motioned to a chair. "Sit down. They're right out of the oven."

"That smell reminds me—" He stopped abruptly.

"Reminds you of what?"

Jake shrugged. "It just . . . just reminds me . . ."

The aroma had taken him back to his grandmother's sunny kitchen, to the array of African violets on the windowsill and the frog cookie jar with one leg badly chipped, to the musical little creak of the oven door just before granny Inez took out the pan of blueberryderries. That was it! It smelled exactly like his Granny's blueberryderries in here!

He sank onto the chair cushion and watched speechlessly as this distant relative of old Maude O'Connor poured milk into a glass, added a sprinkle of cinnamon and popped in a cinnamon stick. She served it with a platter of pastries.

Jake stared at the plate. "Blueberryderries?"

"I beg your pardon?"

He looked at her sheepishly. "These are berryderries!"

"Are you all right, Sheriff MacGuire?" .

He glanced up at her and mumbled, "They're called that."

"Derryberries?"

"No. *Berryder*ries. Blueberryderries." He shook his head and reached for one, took an enormous bite and closed his eyes. The expression on his face was one a woman loves beyond all other, though it's not generally associated with pastry popovers. "I can't believe it," he mumbled, talking to himself.

"Good heavens, it's just a little snack. Here, have some milk."

"You put cinnamon in the milk."

"Yes, is that to your liking?"

"Mmm." He nodded, his mouth very full.

Dana tried to concentrate on the business at hand, but when she looked at this man, all she could see was a calendar page. He'd make the best July she'd ever had—piercing blue eyes, tanned skin, arms with muscles rippling, tight jeans and the gun belt strapped well below the waist. He *was* July—the hottest month of the year.

Another way to bribe him! Of course! She hadn't met a man yet who wasn't flattered when asked to pose. The offer confirmed their own opinion that they were, indeed, hunks. This might work if she played her hand carefully.

In silence, the hunk indulged himself, devouring the rich pastries and sipping milk while Dana watched, and then, as if suddenly remembering where he was, Jake looked across the table at the woman in polka dots. He wiped his mouth with a napkin and said, "My grandmother told me it was a secret recipe brought over from Scotland generations ago. So how could you know it?"

"Oh I . . . just made it up with the ingredients on hand."

He helped himself to another pastry, his fourth. "You mean you've never made these before?"

"No, never."

His voice hardened. "That's kind of unbelievable."

She broke a berryderry in half and took a bite. It was true—they were incredibly delicious. "I don't know why you're making such a big deal out of it." Her gaze

moved to his silver badge. "I was surprised to learn that
the tax assessor is also the sheriff. I've never been in a
room with a man wearing a loaded gun. It is loaded, I
presume."

"What good is an unloaded gun?"

"Surely you don't have occasion to fire it, though. I
mean, except very rarely."

"Does the gun make you nervous?" he asked, his
cheeks full. "Don't worry. It's in a safe place."

She scowled. "When did you last fire that thing?"

"About fifteen minutes ago. Do you always put cinnamon in milk?"

"No, the cinnamon was for you. What do you mean
fifteen minutes ago. You *shot* at somebody?"

"Not directly, no. It was nothing. I didn't shoot anybody, damn it. How could you know I like it?"

"Like to shoot your gun?"

He rolled his eyes. "Like cinnamon milk!"

"I don't know! Who cares about the milk?" She
waited until his mouth was full again to ask, "I was
shocked to get that tax bill. It's nearly thirty thousand
dollars. I don't have that kind of money. You probably
expect to impound the property, is that it? Is that why
you're here?"

He frowned. "You have some options, Miss French.
You could borrow the amount, or you could put the
property up for sale yourself rather than turn it over to
me."

"Why would I borrow the money? I don't live in
Devil's Fork." *Thank God*, she thought. She couldn't
borrow the money because she owed too much on the
mortgage she already had, but her personal financial

affairs were none of his business. "What market value do you put on this house?"

"Maybe fifteen thousand."

"*What?* A taco stand is worth fifteen thousand! You are trying to tax me thirty thousand dollars on property worth—"

"You said market value. The house won't sell for anything but the materials in it. Whoever buys it will tear it down."

Dana was horrified. Aunt Maude could hear this. How dare he say such a thing? Trying to stay calm, she asked, "Why?"

He stirred what was left of the milk with the cinnamon stick. "It's in disrepair and would cost a lot to fix up. Outside people don't move to Devil's Fork, and those who live here are convinced the house is haunted. They're afraid of it."

Dana glanced at the magical glasses on the shelf. "Haunted? How completely silly."

"It's silly, all right. But that's how people are." He looked around. "The inside looks damn nice. I've heard your aunt had impressive antiques."

"Where did you hear that?"

"I have no idea. This town has more hot air than a fleet of balloons. It floats on gossip. Everybody's affairs seem to be everybody else's."

"I hear some bitterness there," she said softly, and thought, *They gossip about him, don't they? And why wouldn't they? A guy who looks like this whom everybody seems to be afraid of?* There *was* something a little intimidating about Sheriff Jake MacGuire, even when his cheeks were puffed out with blueberryderries. His eyes, perhaps.

Jake was not about to let the conversation turn to himself. "The furnishings are worth more than the house. I suggest you sell the house and furnishings separately, pay the taxes, and you'll have a few thousand left over."

"I don't want to sell my aunt's things. She loved them and I love them, too."

"It's your decision. Either we collect the taxes or the town takes possession of the property."

"That's just plain mean!"

The cold blue eyes looked at her. "Your great-aunt didn't pay her property taxes for over forty years. What did you expect? You ought to be grateful the house wasn't confiscated years ago."

"And why wasn't it?"

"Because everybody liked her."

Sure, Dana thought, thankful for the enlightening conversation with his secretary. City officials had been afraid of Maude O'Connor—afraid of what she knew. She must have been camped in the center ring of the gossip circus. Maude and her friends, who were at this moment exerting their power. Through conniving. Through Dana.

"Have another berryderry," she offered demurely, wondering how he could eat so many. He was a big man, but the things were shudderingly rich.

"I think I'm starting to get full."

"Nonsense. Look how many are left."

"I didn't come here to eat," he said, helping himself to another.

Dana poured him a second glass of milk. His eyes followed the movements of her dotted dress. She felt the heat of his stare, sat down again and with her chin in the palm of her hand, studied him. "Forty years' debt, huh?"

He shrugged. "Your aunt liked dogs. When a person likes your dog, you don't turn on them. That's how it is around here."

Her jaw dropped. "When a person likes your *dog?*"

"Dogs matter," he mumbled, chewing.

Her eyes were fixed on the small dimple in his chin. It would be possible to sit here forever just staring at this guy, he was so damned good-looking. She asked, "Do you have a dog?"

"Three dogs."

"I'd like to meet them. I'm a serious dog lover."

This brought a mischievous smile. "Nice try, Miss French."

"Dana." She returned the smile. "You're unfair. I had a Chihuahua once and a bumper sticker that read, 'It's hard to be humble when you own a Chihuahua'." She cleared her throat. "If I've been staring at you, I apologize. It's because you're July. I mean, you should be. July, on a calendar. I am a photographer by profession and I photograph men for calendars. I'd like to photograph you."

He scowled at her, obviously not impressed.

"It has nothing to do with this obscene tax business," she rushed to assure him. "It's strictly business. I photograph working men in their natural environments. I have two requirements, they must be Americans and they can't be professional models. I pay a thousand dollars plus a percentage of sales over fifty thousand. Are you interested?" Of course he was interested. Men always were.

"What the hell are you talking about?"

Was he dense? She rose. "Wait. I'll show you."

She left him sitting amid the blueberryderry crumbs, and hurried up the stairs and returned moments later with her calendars of the past two years.

He flipped over a few pages impatiently. Dana was thinking, *Flattery is the best way to deal with a guy who wants to seize one's house*. "You in your uniform, with the badge and the gun would be splendid. You'd photograph magnificently."

"These are plain weird," he said.

"What?"

"What man would want to pose trying to look like a Greek statue—and have his picture hanging on strangers' walls?"

"Every man I've ever asked, that's who."

"Sure."

Dana bristled, caught off guard by a reaction she had never experienced and hadn't anticipated. "All right, fine. You don't want to be included in a collection of America's most attractive men. Fine. Forget it."

He laid the calendars on the table. "Why are you bringing this up, anyway? We're here to discuss taxes."

"I suppose you think I'm trying to bribe you."

"You said it. I didn't."

"Think what you will. The offer had only to do with my professional eye. Not to worry. I'll find another Colorado man. I like the idea of photographing a rugged Colorado man, with Rocky Mountain peaks in the background."

Her scheme had backfired, and the disappointment was real. He *would* be a perfect subject. He was strong and his aura was powerful.

She could feel the presence of the ghosts around her, watching this strained encounter fearfully. *The house would be torn down!* Words like knives. What were the ghosts telling her to do?

Take control again. Remind him of the mystery, the mystery of her. She picked up the offensive calendars—her proud works of art—and put them aside, and sat down again opposite him. She noticed that he had stopped eating and had gone a little pale. One hand was pressed against his stomach. The blueberryderries must be making him sick, and why wouldn't they? He had eaten at least a dozen.

"Forgive me for deviating from the business at hand," she said, brushing at the pastry crumbs on the table-cloth. "It's just that from the moment I saw you, you reminded me of someone, and I couldn't think who, and then, a few minutes ago I remembered." She flushed. "It's silly, really. You remind me of someone from my childhood."

He was watching her, his face blank. To her chagrin, he didn't ask what memory.

"*Mike of Thunder Mountain*," she volunteered. "It was my favorite book when I was a kid, and you look just like Mike."

He looked as though he had just swallowed castor oil. His lips curled in a most curious scowl and he spoke like someone betrayed. "*Mike of Thunder Mountain?*"

"An adventure book about a boy and his horse. Lightfoot."

"They were just drawings," he said in a strange monotone.

"Oh? You know the book? What a nice coincidence. The drawings were very lifelike, and that kid Mike was just like you. Oh, how I used to dream that I, too, could ride a horse over the Colorado hills. Do you ride?"

He didn't seem to have heard the question. Then, impatiently, he nodded.

"Well, yes, I suppose you would, being a sheriff."

"It's not a well-known book," he said softly. His eyes were filled with questions he could not ask.

She brushed the crumbs into a little mound, then whispered, "I don't want this house torn down."

He did not answer for a long time, until finally, huskily, he said, "I don't think you have a choice."

"It would be a very bad thing to do." She stopped playing with the crumbs and fixed her eyes on his. It was not easy to look into his intimidating eyes, but he was off guard now, as vulnerable as he was likely to get, so she forced herself to hold his gaze.

When she spoke again her voice was low and had an unnatural echo. "If this house were to be torn down, strange things would begin to occur, things the town of Devil's Fork would not like. I don't want to be the person responsible for tearing it down."

He squinted, suddenly alert and defensive. "What is this? Is that some kind of ridiculous threat?"

Maybe she'd gone too far, Dana thought. She'd intended only to scare him into thinking something spooky was going on, because of the blueberryderries and the polka dots and *Mike of Thunder Mountain*. The man might be confused, but he didn't scare.

She answered, "How could I threaten you? It's just . . . this is no ordinary house and it does not wish to be torn down."

"Does not *wish*?"

"I mean, it is a landmark," she said quickly. "Is it not?"

"Not particularly."

"Well, the thing is, it thinks it is. And it's my house now and I don't want it torn down."

He was looking pale, she thought. No question, he was feeling the effects of too many blueberryderries and trying not to show it.

"Maybe you can find another solution, then," he said. "It's not as if anybody else wants this place."

"You mean come up with thirty thousand dollars? But I don't have it."

"What do you suggest we do, then?"

Dana sighed. "Hold off on collecting the taxes, like you did for Maude. We could work out some sort of payment plan."

"I'm not authorized to do that. The town needs the full amount."

"Suddenly, after all these years, it needs the money?"

"That's right." Jake stood. "I can give you two weeks either to come up with the money or put the house on the market. We'll give it six weeks to sell before we impound."

Dana, still seated, was at eye level with his gun. She gazed at it. "You make up your own rules, is that it?"

"That's about it."

She stood up and smoothed the skirt of her dress.

"It's not my fault your great-aunt accumulated such a debt, Miss French."

"It's not my fault, either!" Her shoulders sagged. "Okay, okay, I know it's my responsibility. There must be someone who would buy this house and fix it up to live in. Someone nice."

"Nice?"

"Yes, nice. Someone who would live here for years and years. Happily. There must be a person like that around."

"I doubt it," the sheriff said.

Dana scratched her head. "If I list it at the appraised value, you think somebody will buy it just for the materials? Is that what you said?"

"Yes, with the land. It's probably the best you can do." His hand went to his stomach and he reeled slightly.

"What's the matter?" she asked.

"Nothing."

"Yes, there is. You ate too many blueerryberries."

"Blueberryderries," he corrected, suddenly in a hurry to leave.

With nothing resolved except that the home of the Ladies' Club was going to die! In desperation, Dana reached for the antique glasses and put them on, then picked up a pamphlet and pretended to look at it. The pamphlet, on home remedies for poison, had a large black skull-and-crossbones warning on the cover. Dana barely glanced at it; she was listening to Inez Mac-Guire.

Inez was right beside her, looking proudly and reflectively at her handsome grandson and singing a lullaby. A lovely lullaby, one Dana knew.

"Is there a particular reason you chose this minute to read about poison cures?" Jake demanded, clutching his stomach. "Those derries! What was in them?"

Dana looked up, startled, over the top of the glasses. "Why? Don't you feel well? Those pastries are rich and you ate—my goodness—almost all of them."

"Why is there a pamphlet about poison on the shelf?" Jake said, his face paler than ever.

"How would I know? I just got here." She softened. "But I'm sorry, Jake. May I call you Jake, instead of Sheriff? Sheriff is an awkward first name. Do you want to lie down?"

He looked at her as if she were crazy. "I have to go."

"Why go? You can lie down on the sofa for a bit. I'll fix you bicarbonate of soda to settle your tummy." She took his arm and began to sing the lullaby.

"Sweet and low . . . wind of the western sea . . ."

He looked down at her. "Does eccentricity run in your family, Ms. French?"

"I asked you to call me Dana."

"Were those glasses your aunt's, or do you shop in museums?"

"They were hers. I like old things. Such as this house. And lovely lullabies. Do you know this one?" She kept singing, Granny Inez leading.

"I've heard it," he said distractedly. "First her recipe, now her song."

"Whose?"

He shook his head helplessly. "Never mind."

"I could sing you the whole song while you lie down with a tummy settler. Then you'll feel better."

Her words made him angry. How dare she talk to him like this? *I've got to get out of here*, he thought. *This old house is giving me the creeps*. And why did the actions of this unusually beautiful woman have him flying around in his past? Maybe she had visited her great-aunt years ago when they were children and he had known her then, shared blueberryderries with her, and she remembered and he didn't. But the lullaby? She *couldn't* have known, could she? She was bringing the past out to haunt him, for some manipulative reasons of her own. But why would she want a broken-down old haunted house? She was as eccentric as her aunt.

And yet, there was a gentleness about her that threatened to thaw the ice encasing his heart; he could feel it melting when she sang that lullaby so sweetly, and it took him back to forgotten bedtimes, the sound of rain on the roof at night, mourning doves calling. The song, and the taste of the pastries had filled him with longing for innocent days, long gone and nearly forgotten. Could she have been there some sun-filled summer in the past?

"I have to go," he said.

"If you must. I'll let you know what I decide to do about the house. Meanwhile, perhaps you'd like to come back for more *Berryderries?*"

He didn't reply and let himself out without so much as a thank-you. The door closed hard.

Dana pushed aside the lace curtain and peeked out. Jake MacGuire was leaning over the porch railing, throwing up in the weedy flower bed.

She smiled. So this was the scary, mean sheriff of Devil's Fork. Brought to his knees by pastries and a lullaby.

5

JAKE STAGGERED to the truck and sat for a few moments before starting the engine. Granny Inez had always limited him to three derries; now he knew why. But the churning in his stomach was the least of his concerns. *Who was this woman in polka dots who knew things no stranger could?*

Her eyes were mischievous and full of fire. Full of secrets. And she had a beauty quite unlike any he'd ever seen.

Confused, Jake headed toward home. Behind him the house seemed to stare, as if its windows were eyes. As a kid, he had been afraid of that imposing old house; all the townsfolk were. It was haunted, they said. But ghosts didn't exist. Yet being inside that house was uncomfortable. At one point he had almost imagined he could hear voices where there were none.

There had been only one voice. Dana's.

Her hair had shone in the light from the window, forming a halo of gold as she served up cinnamon milk and blueberryderries and remarks about *Mike of Thunder Mountain*. It had been all he could do to keep his mind on business. He had not felt this attracted to a woman since he'd met Caroline, his wife, more than a decade ago. There had been no one since.

Now thoughts of Dana were heating his blood. It was crazy! She had mesmerized him as no woman ever had.

"God help me," Jake mumbled to himself. "I don't know what to make of her."

When he turned into the drive of his ranch-style house, his dogs ran out to greet him, tails flapping wildly. Three bandits, he called them—a German shepherd, a bloodhound and a terrier mix. Jake was standing in the yard, with tails pounding against his legs and dirty paw marks on his jeans, when the mayor's new car purred up the gravel driveway.

"Nice evening," Russell said as he got out. "I thought I'd stop by for a beer." He sat down in a chair on the front porch and propped his feet on the railing.

"Be right with you," Jake said, heading inside.

He filled three dog bowls with dog food and took two beers from the refrigerator. Russell didn't make a habit of stopping by. There was some reason, and Jake had an idea what it was.

The screen door squeaked as he returned.

"I heard you had an appointment with Maude O'Connor's heir," Russell began as soon as he heard the door.

Jake handed him a beer and sat down. "Don't start counting the thirty thousand yet. She says she doesn't have it. Even if she does, she has no intention of paying."

"I was afraid of that."

"Hell, we knew that. Who's going to want to pay twice what the house is worth in taxes?" He propped his boots up on the railing beside Russell's and sighed.

"So what is she going to do, then? Turn it over to us?"

"I don't know. She seems to want the house."

"*Want* it?" Russell yelped. "For what? It'll just stand empty. Nobody'll rent it."

Jake shrugged. "I don't know. She has some sentimental attachment to it. My guess is she'll sell because she has no choice, and she'll have to let it go for almost nothing."

"There'll be no buyer in Devil's Fork."

"We know that, but she doesn't."

Russell gulped the beer and belched. "You wouldn't catch me staying in that house. It's haunted as hell. What'd you think of her? Nellie Jean met her in your office and said she's foxy, but God forbid I should get excited about Nellie Jean's opinion of any woman."

"Dana French makes the women around here look dowdy."

Russell grinned. "That right? A city girl? And wanting that house? Is she playing some kind of game?"

"I don't know. I gave her two weeks."

"That's too long, Cuz. I want that money now."

"For God's sake, it's been delinquent forty years!"

Russell scratched the ears of the hound and took another gulp of his beer. "It's more than a matter of taxes, Jake. There's a lien against the O'Connor house."

Jake shook his head. "You're mistaken. I've seen nothing like that. Who has a lien?"

"I have. Maude borrowed three thousand dollars from me once. I put a legal lien on the property when I knew she couldn't pay back the loan."

Jake sat up. "Why the hell didn't you tell me this, Russ? Those papers aren't on public record!"

"They are now. To be honest, I forgot until today."

"Well, that's just great! So Dana French actually owes more like thirty-three thousand, plus interest on your loan."

"That's it." Russell pulled a cigarette from his pocket and lit up. "But I'm willing to buy the house."

"What would you do that for?"

"I wouldn't mind having the land."

Jake scowled. "You have got enough cash to buy it, have you?"

"I can raise fifteen thousand. She'll have to make up the rest of it. I hear Maude's antique collection is worth bucks."

"You sound like a damn vulture," Jake said, disgusted.

"Hell, it's our money. This French gal just happened on to it, and I expect to get what we're owed." He drew hard on his cigarette and blew out a great circle of smoke. "So you tell her that I, as holder of the lien, am not willing to dance around. Tell her I'd like to make an offer on the house."

Jake wanted to say, "Tell her yourself," but he didn't because he wanted to see her again. He was hopelessly drawn to her. Besides, he wanted to determine whether her concern about the house was genuine or a stall. Not that it would matter, because Russ was ready to pounce, and the mayor of Devil's Fork always got what he wanted.

Ross wanted Maude O'Connor's property dirt cheap. But what would a Texas girl do with it? She was lucky to get Russ for a buyer; the property could stay unsold for years.

The mayor looked at him. "You're not drinking your beer. Come on. Let's go to the Coyote Inn for a T-bone steak."

Jake's stomach did a turn. "You go on. I'm not hungry."

"What? You're always hungry! You're a bottomless pit."

"Tonight I'm not hungry. I already ate."

"Where?"

"If I told you you wouldn't believe it." If he so much as mentioned the blueberryderries to Russell, his cousin would be at Dana's faster than a scared rabbit could run. He didn't want smooth-talking Russell over there moving in on territory Jake already considered his.

"I had a snack," he said. "I don't want any dinner."

Jake looked out at pale pink sky turning orange as the sun sank in the west. In the distance a bobwhite sang and in the grass crickets chirped after the heat of the day. His favorite time of day was also the most lonely. Having his cousin here didn't help.

For some reason, Jake was more keenly aware tonight of the emptiness in his life.

SITTING IN THE LIVING room surrounded by ghosts should have made Dana uncomfortable, but it didn't. The ghosts were now her friends.

"It was so good to see Jake again," Inez was saying.

"My word but he's handsome," Rosella remarked.

"Yet still so troubled," Jake's grandmother sighed.

"We have a frightening problem here," Maude reminded them. "What happens to us if this house is destroyed? Where will we go? How will we stay together?"

Frances dabbed at her eyes with a lace handkerchief. "The house cannot be destroyed, it simply can*not!*"

Dana said sadly, "The only hope is to convince Jake to take payments over time, and I'll have to find a way to make those payments."

Louise spoke up. "But the mayor wants to finish the swimming pool this summer and there's no other revenue." She turned to Dana. "He insisted on buying that dog statue, and it cost so much there's no money for the pool. They can't even borrow it because—" she looked around at the others in dismay "—because the town's credit is no longer worth a cent. What a disgrace! If *we* were running things, it would be a different story."

"Unfortunately we are not running things," Maude said. "Dana is our only hope. Think, girls, think!"

"The blueberryderries made him sick," Dana said.

"Ah, and also very confused." Inez smiled. "And for the first time in his life he was able to consume as many as he wanted. Maybe now he'll appreciate his granny's restraints."

Dana sighed heavily. "He is a hard case. I thought if he posed for me I'd have a chance to flatter him and make him more approachable. I can work wonders with my camera. I couldn't believe he turned down my offer. No man has ever turned down a chance to pose for me—male egos being what they are." She chewed on her thumbnail, exasperated. "Jake obviously has an ego, too, but of a different sort. He seems so sure of himself, and yet . . . the way he reacted—or tried not to react—to his childhood memories showed his sentimental side. Reaching it, though—that's the challenge."

"Nevertheless, we must get him to accept tax in payments," determined Evelyn. "We have to work on him harder. What else can you tell us about him, Inez? Think! We need a plan!"

The phone rang. Dana, who was sitting cross-legged on the brocaded sofa, uncurled herself as if from a trance and limped into the kitchen with a cramp in her left leg.

It was Jake. She knew it would be.

"Something has come up," he said. "I'll be out tomorrow to talk about it."

"Is it bad news? You don't sound very good. Or are you not feeling well? I'm awfully sorry about your stomach."

He didn't want to talk about his stomach. "It isn't very encouraging news, Dana."

It was interesting that he didn't ask her to come to his office in town. Was he hoping she'd be baking again tomorrow?

"Can't you tell me?"

"I'd rather wait until I can check the records to be sure of my facts. Meanwhile, do you want the name of a realtor?"

"No. I told you I don't want to sell."

"We'll talk about it tomorrow. I'll come by around five."

"You might ask if the time is convenient."

"I might. But since you don't know a soul in this town, I don't expect your social calendar is full. However, I will ask, if you like. Is five o'clock convenient?"

"Yes. I've just checked my calendar and it is."

"Fine." He hesitated. Then, "Dana?"

"Yes?"

"Are you all right?"

She gave a start. "What do you mean?"

His voice was halting. "I mean, it's getting dark, and you haven't been in that house at night. Will you be okay?"

"Is this about ghosts, Jake?"

He was slow to answer. "Well, there *are* stories. If you get scared you can call me."

"I won't get—" she began, and then stopped. *He wants to feel like a hero even if he doesn't want to pose to look as one for a photograph. Play along.*

"I appreciate the offer. There are some creaks and groans, but I'll be okay, I'm sure I will . . ."

"Take my number down, anyway. I live up the road just a couple of miles." He gave her the number, which she wrote on the little apple-shaped pad beside the telephone.

She asked, "But surely you don't *believe* the ghost stories? You said you didn't. You said they were silly."

"I think you said they were silly and I agreed with you. I just meant, if you need me . . ."

He was worried; she could tell. And he wasn't at all sure he didn't believe in ghosts. Not when the whole town was convinced this house was haunted. The ladies of the club had not been as subtle as they thought.

She said, "Thanks for your concern."

"See you tomorrow, then," he replied, and rang off.

They were all in the living room when Dana returned, but she knew they'd be in the kitchen listening to every word. She looked from one to another. "Tell me, do bad ghosts—I mean the scary kind—exist?"

"Of course," replied Rosella. "Mean people become mean ghosts. It takes more than a simple death to change somebody."

"What does it take to change somebody?"

"It takes true and forever love to make a soul kind."

I am sitting here calmly philosophizing with ghosts, Dana thought. It was incredible, yet strangely natural. "Why am I privileged to know all of you? To talk to you and learn these secret things? Is it because you need my help?"

"Yes, but it's more than need," Maude said. "It is because you loved me. Even though I saw you so seldom, I felt your love."

Tears formed in Dana's eyes. "It was true, I did—do—love you very much. But the others . . ."

"The others are my family now," Maude said. "And therefore *your* family, taking the place of the family you lost at such a young age. Now you have us, who love you."

"On this side of the thin line," Louise continued, "love is not rationed as it is in your realm. It is like the air you breathe. We love you and want to help you as much as you want to help us—now that you are one of us."

"One of our family, that is," Frances qualified.

Dana blinked backed tears. She had felt that love everywhere in this house—in every crack and corner of this wonderful house!

"There has to be a way to save this place!" she said, wiping the moisture from her cheek with a clenched, determined fist. "Jake would do it if he could."

"Think, girls!" Maude said.

"Jake is worried about Dana," Inez said, "which is in character—rather, his old, natural character. A good sign our plan is working. First off, we'll make chicken and dumplings tomorrow. And chocolate cake with coconut for dessert—his favorite. Not to worry—I am—was—the best cook in the county. Dana is now." She rubbed her thin hands together. "Poor Jake. He's been alone too long. It breaks my heart to see him drifting like this."

"Drifting like what?" Dana asked. "I don't understand why you speak about your grandson with such sadness."

Evelyn quickly brushed off Dana's concern. "Just nostalgia. Now. Where were we? Oh, yes, Dana must learn all the words to that lullaby. The song affected Jake more than he'd admit."

"But no matter how softened up he gets, he said he didn't have the authority to allow me to pay the taxes over time." *There is something about him they haven't told me,* she thought. *Some subject they keep skirting—the reason the sheriff is adrift and alone.*

"He has the final say in all tax matters," Rosella declared. "That's his job." She dangled one shoe on her toe as a young woman might. "The tax assessor before Jake was Willie Saint, but Willie was no saint, was he, girls? Oh, my, no. All the girls in school knew him as Willie the Conqueror."

"Never mind that now," Louise cut in impatiently.

"Why is Willie no longer the tax man?" Dana asked.

Maude replied, "Russell chose his cousin when he became mayor. So we're stuck with Jake, who can't be bribed. The best we can hope for is to weaken him—which is a precarious plan if all we have to work with are dumplings and cake."

"We will have to break him down slowly," Inez said. "At least until we think of a grand play."

"Grand play?"

Inez looked at Maude's niece. "I know my grandson well enough to recognize reactions hidden under that tough exterior. He didn't look at you the way a tax collector looks at an outstanding balance. No. He looked at you the way a man looks at a woman."

The remark caused Dana's knees to grow weak, but she wasn't about to admit it. What if he did find her attractive? The thought excited her beyond all reason. She could still feel the heat of his eyes—cold eyes generating heat! *If you need me,* he had said. *If you need me.* Do I need this crazy haunted dot on the map called Devil's Fork? Do I need a sullen stranger galloping through my life, my perfect, independent life? Dana tried to blink her thoughts away. Her heart, with desires of its own, was argumentative. *Don't you need a man to hold you? Sometimes in the night? Sometimes in the winter chill?*

She sighed and settled back on the sofa, forgetting that anyone—any mortal—looking into this room would see a lone young woman conversing with herself. She wanted Inez to tell her about Jake Mac-Guire—not just to build a plot against him, but because she wanted to know. The man fascinated her. She wanted to know every cute, sad, funny little thing, just for the knowing. She wanted to figure out why this good-looking man had refused to pose for her. A man who didn't try to be sexy was the sexiest of all.

"What was he like as a child?" she asked Inez. "When he wasn't being a human slingshot or sleeping with his teddy bear?"

"He was naughty." The old woman smiled. "I recall a time when he and Russell were playing a game with their red wagon. The idea was that one would get into the wagon and cover up with a towel and the other would pull him around, then the one inside had to guess where he was when the wagon stopped." She giggled. "Jake's father's dogs had killed a coyote and he had hung the carcass in a tree to show Russell's father how clever his dogs were. The carcass got pretty ripe. Jake pulled the wagon directly under the maggot-infested thing, and when Russell pulled the towel away, his arms shot out in terror and half the rotted carcass fell right on him. Jake laughed so hard he fell backward into a creek. Russell swore revenge and never forgave him."

"Did Russell ever get his revenge?" Frances asked.

"Not that I'm aware of. The two had plenty of fights through the years."

"Jake had a bad poison ivy attack when he was a lad," Inez went on. "Is that the sort of thing you want to know?"

"I want to know why you said he's adrift."

"He's unhappy without a wife."

Rosella looked from Dana to Inez and back again, the way she did when she was dying to talk but needed the others' approval. "He had a wife once, you know. She was killed when her car slid on the ice and went down an embankment. There were a lot of rumors about that accident. People said she was in love with another man and he was with her in the car, and that he ran off and left her there, scared of what would happen when Jake found out."

Dana gasped and turned to her great-aunt. "Jake's wife was killed? *Was* she in love with another man?"

"There is no doubt that Jake believes it, even though people said he never explained why he was so sure."

Incredible, Dana thought. Incredible that any woman would turn away from a man like Jake MacGuire.

"Jake was devastated when she died, but he was also furious," Frances put in. "Rumors had it he swore he'd find out who the man was and get revenge."

"And he didn't?"

"He's never found him," Rosella said. "And he's still so bitter he won't have anything to do with women." She looked around. "Isn't that so, girls?"

They nodded sadly in unison.

"It's been seven years," Inez offered. "Long enough for him to be over it. But he can't put the matter to rest, so determined is he to find that man."

Dana studied the ghost. "That's why he's adrift?"

"Yes. He is mistrustful and unhappy because no man is truly happy without a wife. Especially Jake. He ought to be married."

Dana listened in anguish as the ghosts spoke so casually of the mysterious death of a woman Jake had once loved. It was easy for ghosts to speak casually of death—not so easy for her to absorb what they had just told her about Jake's life. Outside it had grown very dark.

What did he do at night, she wondered, picturing his face in firelight on a winter evening. Or on a summer's night, like tonight. Was he alone? He'd offered to protect her from ghosts he didn't believe in, but he could hardly protect her from the unsettling curiosity she was feeling about him. Here she was, surrounded by the phenomenon of visible, talking ghosts, and her thoughts returned doggedly to an arrogant lawman whose very voice caused her heart to betray her. There had to be plenty of other women equally affected by the sheriff's deep voice and blue eyes and reluctant smile.

I'm not going to get in line for a crumb of his affection, Dana determined with gritted teeth. *That's probably what he expects, but I'm not going to do it.*

Even as the voice inside her made those vows, Dana was thinking ahead to the sight of him standing once again in her doorway. Tomorrow.

6

DANA WAS AWARE of the clock all day. The ticking seconds mocked her in the kitchen while she ploughed headlong into Inez's cooking lessons, surrounded by cheerleaders who spoke in soft echoes. Sifting flour, measuring oil, beating eggs, cutting chicken—these were not natural moves for Dana, who was not at home in a kitchen unless she was in front of a microwave with a packaged frozen dinner.

The ticking seconds mocked her in her bedroom while she tried to decide what to wear. Polka dots had been done. Now what?

"Pink silk and lace," Maude suggested. "Men can't resist pink silk."

"The only pink silk I own is a shirt. Forget lace. I don't generally pack lace for appointments with tax assessors." She pulled the silk shirt from the drawer. "Okay. I'll wear this." She tucked the shirt into her tight jeans, and turned in front of the mirror.

Rosella approved. "Good. Hurry up. It's almost five! The sheriff is never late."

"Unless he's out shooting something or someone," Dana corrected. She slid into her gold-chain sandals, ran a brush through her hair and checked her careful makeup.

"A little more perfume," Maude said.

"I'm already reeking!"

Evelyn laughed. "Reeking is good."

"If this scheme doesn't work," Frances, the practical one, said, "if he won't accept payments on the taxes, what is to become of us? And even if Dana does soften him up, who is going to live in the house and maintain it? It looks, girls, as if our sanctuary might be doomed."

Deadly silence hovered, for Frances had stated what the others were afraid to. Dana felt a small, dizzy chill. Was it inside her, that chill, or was it in the air?

She said weakly, "I'll find someone to buy the house. But right now, it's the tax guy we have to worry about. We'll have to go one step at a time." She turned to Inez. "I hope those dumplings are as effective as the blueberryderries."

"Trust me," Jake's grandmother said. "In some respects I know this man better than he knows himself. But the dumplings alone can't do it, dear. The rest is up to you."

"To me," Dana acknowledged with a glance in the mirror. She had never been a seductress, was no good at it. But then, she'd never had this kind of ammunition to work with either—secret tips from a ghost.

Or this kind of incentive. Incentive that wasn't a hundred percent to do with the saving of Aunt Maude's house. Sheriff Jake MacGuire was challenge with a capital C. One of the few men whose eyes could mesmerize and whose smile—rationed though it was— could melt the strongest woman's defenses.

Dana didn't like her defenses melted; she was too used to being in control. The men she photographed often wanted to date her, but she kept her distance. The two whom she had let closer were both selfish. Dana had believed, for a time, she loved them. But neither had allowed her to be herself—not John with his jealousy of her work, nor Walt with his unwelcome interference in it.

Men, Dana had concluded, were controlling because they were so vulnerable. The sheriff was vulnerable in ways even he did not understand. She had seen him soften over happy childhood memories, as his grandmother had said he would. This man, who was so angry over the past, was also a sad man. And a lonely man.

THE CLOCK on the parlor wall chimed its final little jeer at the same time the doorbell rang. Dana opened the door to blue eyes that were not as cold as before.

Jake blinked at the sight of his hostess in shadowy pink silk with the hint of a lace bra showing through and jeans molded to her hips like pale blue clay. Seconds teased by before he spoke, seconds during which he was without words and Dana knew it.

She felt heat radiating from him and from herself, the chemistry between them smoldering in the warm, thick air, working like those vials bubbling with mysterious substances threatening to explode. But when he spoke, it was not the explosion she expected.

"Orange Nights," he said.

"Close enough."

"No, I like to get things right." He moved closer and sniffed. "What, then?"

"Night of an Orange Moon."

"It's not like me to forget a moon."

She stood aside for him to enter. Jake walked past her into the foyer which opened into the wide hall, and said,

"My grandmother used to tell me the Colorado moon is brighter and bigger than any other moon."

"Maybe it's all in the beholding,"

He sniffed at the aromas drifting down the hallway from the kitchen.

Quickly Dana stepped in front of him. "I realized you were coming from work and wouldn't have had dinner. So I made up something for you to eat."

"I don't expect to be fed. I've just come on business."

When his hand moved involuntarily over his stomach, Dana knew he was wondering whether his system could take it. One would think he'd been *forced* to gorge himself yesterday.

"Oh, I didn't make more of those derry treats. I've prepared something more substantial. I hope you like chicken and dumplings."

"Ah, that's what smells so good." He followed her down the long hallway to the kitchen.

"Smells better than Night of an Orange Moon?" She felt his eyes on her body, and aware of the tightness of her jeans and the seductive sheen of pink, Dana tossed back her hair like a temptress. But how effective was a temptress with trembling knees and a recurring blush?

"I can't honestly say it smells better than Orange Moon Night," Jake said, "but I repeat, I didn't come to eat."

His protest was weak and unconvincing. The dumplings—perhaps combined with the extra swing in her hips—were working their spell. "Don't be so stuffy, sheriff. It's Texas hospitality."

"Or friendly persuasion. I already said I don't have good news for you about the tax situation."

He can do about it whatever he chooses, the ghosts had told her. She said, "I doubt the news could be any worse than yesterday. Are you accusing me of trying to bribe you with dumplings?"

"Aren't you?"

Dana laughed. "'Bribe' is an awfully strong word. The way I was brought up, one cannot have a guest at supper time without supper."

"I'm not a guest," he said mildly as they entered the kitchen and his eyes came to rest on the two-layered chocolate cake. This woman had made a cherry face on the cake exactly like his grandmother used to do. What the hell was going on here?

"Is something the matter? You do like chocolate-cherry cake, don't you?"

"You must have known my grandmother," he muttered.

"That's an odd thing to say."

"She—my grandmother—used to put faces on her cakes."

She smiled. "Oh. Well, why not? Faces are cute. Pull up a chair while I check on the dumplings. I don't want to hear your bad news, but I suppose I'll have to. Ah, but have a drink first. I'll split a beer with you."

He was staring at the polka-dot napkins on a table set with white dishes and white candles in blue glass holders. "I think you might be a lady with incredible intuitive powers."

Dana shrugged innocently, poured beer into two chilled glasses, set one down before him and watched him drink thirstily before she lit the candles. She sat across from him, aware of how candlelight danced on the pink sheen of her blouse. Whatever his bad news was, she didn't want to hear it. Better to try to deflect the blow. She asked sweetly, "Have you given some thought to letting me pay off the taxes in installments?"

"I'm afraid that's out of the question."

Her heart sank. "Is the city that desperate?"

"Yeah. But it's more than that. I found out the mayor holds a lien on this house."

Dana felt blood drain from her face. "What? How could you not have known this before?"

"It wasn't in the public records. Russell—that's the mayor—told me just last night. He has a lien because of money he lent Maude O'Connor, and he wants the property."

"This sounds very strange! Does he want to live here?"

"Of course not, but since he has the lien, he's decided he wants the land around and under the house."

She swallowed. "He would tear it down?"

"Yeah. He'll offer what the land is worth. The house has little market value, as I already told you. You could try to find another buyer, but you won't have any luck. Russ intends to foreclose, and he can, with that tax debt."

Dana rose, feeling the unseen presence of the ladies of the club, feeling their horror and their fear.

At the stove, she lifted the lid from the simmering pot and said, "The mayor is your cousin. His secretary told me that when I was at the courthouse yesterday. Have you any influence over your cousin?"

"Not when it comes to money matters." He sat back in the chair. "I hate to be the bearer of bad news, Dana. It looks like you'll have to let the house go. I can't fathom why you'd want the place, anyhow. You wouldn't live in it."

"I would if I were a resident of Devil's Fork, but my home and work are in Dallas." She began to ladle out the dumplings. "I don't see why you're so sure it wouldn't sell. It's a beautiful old house."

"It needs a lot of repairs." He shifted self-consciously. "I take it you haven't seen any sign of a ghost?"

"Do I look like the sort of person who sees ghosts?" She set a steaming plate in front of him. "How did these rumors get started, anyhow? Did somebody see something?"

"I have no idea." He was gazing at his plate. "This looks fantastic."

"It *is* fantastic. So is this. My special recipe for squash and corn."

He stared at the dish of vegetables. "Yellow squash and . . . I don't believe it, Dana, I just don't. Something mighty strange is going on here."

"I don't know what you mean. Please help yourself to the vegetables."

He looked up, lost. "It goes beyond coincidence. You seem to have a way of knowing all the things I used to— all the things I like. Who have you been talking to?"

She looked insulted. "Talking about what?"

"About me."

"I assure you, Jake MacGuire, I haven't been talking to a living soul since I set foot in this house yesterday afternoon."

He took a generous helping of squash and corn. "Are you sure you haven't been talking to somebody?"

"Not a living soul, I told you. Why? Is there something I should know that I don't?"

He ate in silence for a few moments, savoring every bite. "I wonder if there is *anything* you don't know."

Dana watched him eat, thinking even the way he ate was sensual. The movements of his lips and jaw were distracting, almost mesmerizing. Better not to look at his lips. Better not to look at his eyes, either. Hell, she was even aware of his *breathing*. She struggled to bring her thoughts back to the sticky problem at hand. "I want to pay off the taxes in small installments."

"It's impossible with the lien."

She squinted. "In other words, it's the mayor who has the say in this, not you."

"That's right. And unlike myself, I doubt Russell would succumb to blueberryderries and dumplings."

Her voice grew hard. "You are accusing me of bribery."

He laughed, chewing diligently. "A lawman is a trained psychologist. I've been bribed with everything from watermelon jelly to pumpkin pancakes to homegrown fishing worms. It makes people happy to bribe me, even though it never works. I'll have to admit, though, that blueberryderries and chicken dumplings and a clown-face cake have gotten my attention. Enough to want to help if I could. Hell, too bad I can't."

Homegrown fishing worms? And she thought pastries were original. How did one act incensed when the urge—in spite of the dire situation—was to burst out laughing? Dana managed to keep a straight face. "I offer my Southern hospitality and you insult me by calling it bribery. I'm appalled."

Jake chuckled and wiped his chin. "Appalled, huh? What I'm wondering is why. Why would you try so hard to keep this broken-down old house?"

"It can be renovated!"

"By you, who live in Dallas?"

"It's . . . sentimental."

"Sure. You've been here so often and all."

Anger welled up in Dana. He was telling her the house was already lost to a man who planned to tear it down. He and his cousin were bullying her and she didn't like it.

"First the taxes, now the lien. I feel as if you and the mayor are pulling me around in a wagon with a towel over my head so I can't see what's really going on."

Jake's head snapped up as if she'd pulled it by a rope. A bite of dumpling fell from his fork. He scowled. "You've been here before, haven't you? As a little kid. You've been in the wagon with the towel and in Granny's kitchen."

Dana lowered her eyes and answered innocently, "I don't know what you're talking about."

"Have you known me before?"

"Have you been in Dallas?"

"No." Jake wiped his chin with the dotted napkin, eager to change the subject. "Look, I told you, I didn't know about the damn lien, but I couldn't agree to payments, anyway, because the town feels it's waited for its money long enough."

"You're trying to scare me off. I think you've got a dead coyote hidden up some tree."

This last remark was too much for him. Wagons and dead coyotes—she was picking at old memories. He set his napkin on the table and stood up, angry and confused. "Dana, I have to go."

"But you haven't had any cherry-face cake."

He glanced at the cake the way one might look at a weapon of war. Dana thought, *Whoops, I might have gone too far with the dead coyote remark. He looks like a man afraid of being poisoned.*

And then she thought, *What difference does it make? Nothing is going to make him bend.*

"Thank you for the dinner," Jake said, inching toward the hall. "Hospitable of you. Sorry I had to bring bad news, but I can't for the life of me understand why you'd want to hang on to this place." He lifted one eyebrow. "Maybe there's something you're not telling *me.*"

Dana followed him toward the door, not knowing how to answer. She had overdone it and scared him away. So much for seduction, and just as she was getting used to the dimple in his cheek when he smiled and the rich tones of his dark hair in the window light. The man might be impossibly stubborn, but he was fabulous to look at. She imagined him behind the lens of her camera. The thought of him posing in an open shirt, seducing the camera lens with his eyes, made her tremble so badly she tripped over an edge of the Persian runner in the hallway and fell back against the wall with a clumsy thud. One of her sandals went flying.

He reached out to catch her. She felt the heat of his touch through the silk of her sleeve, and then his hand in hers like fire meeting fire. Her face went scarlet. She forced herself out of his grip and shuffled to retrieve her sandal, which had landed in front of the door. So much for the seductive walk she thought she'd perfected.

Jake had felt the heat of her body penetrating his hand, almost like a burn. The hot silk was soft—like a woman's softness. And the flush in Dana's cheeks was not unlike a woman's flush of passion. . . .

Rattled, Jake straightened and could not look at her. His voice was thick. "Let me know your decision." He made no pretense about his eagerness to get out of there.

Standing in the open doorway, she watched the sheriff rush down the front steps. Too much probing at his past had only served to spook him. The dumplings had not reached his conscience.

She walked dispiritedly back into the kitchen and put on the eyeglasses. Her heart felt as heavy as lead. The ladies gathered around as she slumped into his vacated chair and pushed aside his almost empty plate. "It's hopeless!"

"It can't be hopeless! The house can't be lost!" Rosella wailed. "Inez, has your grandson no heart?"

"In his defense," Dana said, "it makes no sense to him, and how could it? These things I know about him aren't softening him as much as giving him the creeps."

Frances began to pace. "Something *has* to be done!" She stopped beside the chair. "My dear, we cannot leave this house. You are our only link to the outside world— the only one who can do it."

Dana crumpled deeper into the chair. "Do what?"

"We don't know what," Maude said. "Think, girls! We could get *anything* accomplished once."

Dana said, "Tell me about Mayor Russell Mac-Guire. What sort of man is he?"

"He was a very naughty child," Inez answered. "Jake was naughty, too, but Jake wasn't overly mean. Russell would stop at almost nothing to get what he wanted. He was capable of hurting other children. If he has decided he wants the house, I don't think even Jake can stop him."

"He was elected to public office, so he must be popular."

"Yes, he is," Louise put in. "He is a charming and persuasive man. Everyone likes him, but people don't try to cross him, like they don't cross Jake."

"Our mayor isn't married," Maude volunteered. "He was until his wife went to Omaha. No one knew what was wrong, but rumors were he was having an affair. Women find Russell attractive."

"The cousins must be quite a pair," Dana mused, staring at the reflection of her pink blouse on the side of a polished teapot. She could still feel the sensation of Jake's hand on her arm. And the sting of his hasty exit. "It sounds like Russell is more receptive to women than Jake."

"No question about that," Inez confirmed. "You must meet him dear, try to persuade him. It's our only chance."

Dana straightened. "Women find him attractive? Does he look anything like Jake?"

"No," Evelyn said. "Not like Jake. But Russell is a handsome man, anyone would say so."

"Then maybe there is a way. I'll go meet him. I'll make an appointment for tomorrow morning."

Maude was pacing in front of the stove. "The last I heard he was dating the oldest Collins girl from Eversville. The mayor's life is active. We ought to have the latest scoop on him, but we don't."

"We have had no outside link since Maude crossed over," Rosella explained. "It's terrible. How are we supposed to keep up with what's going on? Dana, you could do it! Have your hair done at Marylee's Beauty

Shop! Then you can fill us in on everything that's happening in Devil's Fork!"

"The perfect idea!" Louise agreed. "Oh, Dana, we've been dying to learn all the latest gossip!"

"Dying to?" Frances chortled, and they all dissolved in giggles.

This bunch was unbelievable. At the prospect of getting the latest gossip, the ghosts were so excited they began dancing around. Three of them were humming in unison—an eerie sound. Dana was skeptical. "What makes you think anyone will confide in a stranger?"

Maude considered this. "We shall make you an insider by giving you something juicy to pass along. Something intriguing about me would do. Let's see..."

"I don't want to spread dreadful stories."

The giggling resumed. Maude said, "Goodness, it's not as if I've ever minded being thought of as eccentric. It's certainly preferable to dull. Now, girls, what tale shall we invent?"

The group had become greatly animated; the ladies were once again doing what they did best.

"Let's give you a secret past," Rosella suggested. "Yes, good! A secret lover who brought you a single red rose every Christmas Eve for decades!"

Dana scowled. "I once saw that in a movie."

"Besides," Maude said, "once a year is not enough. I want more passion than that in my secret life."

"You had a lover who came in the dark of night and always slipped away before morning..." Louise began.

"...because he was the husband of another woman in town who shall remain nameless," continued Rosella.

The giggling became uncontrolled.

"Perfect!" Frances whooped. "Let every woman look at her husband and wonder if he's the one."

Horrified, Dana objected. "That's awful!"

"Yes, isn't it?" agreed two delighted ghosts in unison.

Seeing them in their element, Dana understood why this group had power when they were organized and working together. The Ladies' of the Club was just plain dangerous and its members all knew it and thrived on their subversive mischief.

"Have your hair done first," Frances was saying, "so that when you go to see Russell, you'll be armed with the latest talk. There is always gossip about him and his cousin. Any comment on the MacGuire men will boot it up." She grinned proudly. "Boot it up. That's computer language."

Rosella scowled at her friend. "You always brag about that time you used a computer. I'm tired of hearing 'boot it up' every time we start talking." She turned her plump face toward Dana. "Nevertheless, boot it up is what you do. Mention that Jake was at your house two evenings in a row and be extremely vague as to why. That'll start the gossip percolating."

I don't want any part of this, Dana wanted to say, but it wasn't true. Not when she saw how delighted the ladies were at the prospect of catching up on the town gossip. Spying for them would be fun.

And maybe useful, she thought. The mayor of Devil's Fork was only a man. He could be dealt with. A mayor, after all, wouldn't be sullen like a certain sheriff. Russell might be easier to manipulate. Depending on how determined he was to get this haunted house away from her.

7

DANA SAT IN HER CAR in the parking lot of Marylee's Beauty Shop on the main street of Devil's Fork, frantically trying to brush some of the frizzled curls out of her hair. "I look like I'm wearing seaweed," she wailed aloud. What a great way to impress the town's highest official.

In the mirror she caught the reflection of two people passing by and turned in alarm. A masked bandit was walking with an Indian in a feathered headdress, except on closer inspection, the Indian was not an Indian, but a middle-aged white man wearing war paint. Even more alarming was the fact that no one was paying the slightest attention to the bandit and the Indian impersonator. What kind of crazy town *was* this?

She gave up trying to undo the damage Marylee had done to her hair, put down the brush, took a small notebook out of her handbag and began making notes on the gossip she'd heard in the beauty salon while it was still fresh in her mind. It was being whispered that a certain Miss Helen Gunn was claiming to have accepted the marriage proposal of Mayor Russell MacGuire, yet Russell had been seen at a picnic in the next county with a different woman on his arm only last weekend. The sheriff, it seems, was asked to the same picnic by a Jean Hardy and turned down the invitation. Gossip bore out the fact that Jake was antisocial. Russell was the charmer-about-town.

Remembering the stir she herself had caused in the shop, Dana smiled to herself. Before she even got out the door, speculation was gathering like storm clouds among the clients as to the identity of Maude O'Connor's lover. They had reacted to Dana's story like waddling, quacking ducks racing toward crumbs of bread. This was so juicy, even talk about the MacGuire cousins was cut off in midstream.

Two blocks away was the courthouse where she had an eleven-o'clock appointment. It was two minutes to eleven now. Dana closed her notebook and started the car.

In the office of the mayor, Nellie Jean Schrock stood behind her desk, pacing and talking impatiently on the telephone. Her hair was tucked up inside a battered old rimmed hat. She wore an oversize man's shirt that looked like a reject from a secondhand store, and baggy pants, held up by a knotted rope.

"I'll look up all those figures tomorrow," she said abruptly, and set down the phone as she looked up. "Dana! So you've survived two nights in that big old house!"

Dana tried not to stare at the woman's outrageous outfit. "I have an eleven-o'clock appointment."

Nellie Jean scratched her head. "Omigod, you have? I thought it was for tomorrow. We're all tied up here."

"It was definitely for today. I must see Mayor MacGuire."

The woman pushed back a lock of dark hair that had fallen from under her hat. "The Town Players are here right now. Our Devil's Fork Actors' Guild. The mayor called a rehearsal because he's located a new dog to take the part of our founding hero, Brutus, and this new Brutus must familiarize himself with his part in the play."

Dana remembered the statue of the regal German shepherd in the town square. "You are a member of the Town Players, I presume," she said, certain it would do little good to express indignation that her appointment had been ignored because of a play rehearsal for the benefit of a dog.

"I play Jeremiah, the driver of the second wagon." She studied Dana. "You're not familiar with the story of the founding of our town? Well, Lordy! Stay and watch our rehearsal."

At this point, a tornado couldn't have stopped Dana from staying. She asked, "Where is Mayor MacGuire?"

"Oh, he's the current lead in the play! Of *course.*" Nellie Jean winked and motioned for Dana to follow her through the double doors to the mayor's private office. Inside, an enormous Town Players sign was propped against one wall. The bandit was lighting a cigarette for the Indian impersonator. Women in pioneer dresses and bonnets were rearranging furniture while three children who looked like fugitives from "Bonanza" bounced a ball. A man dressed like Nellie Jean was carrying a card that said, "Driver Number Three," and an arrogant boxer dog strutted among the actors sniffing rudely at everybody.

"A boxer?" Dana asked. "I thought Brutus was a German shepherd."

Nellie Jean smiled. "The truth is, we have no idea what breed he was. The mayor *likes* this dog, and whatever the mayor likes, he gets. Especially since his ancestor—Penrose MacGuire—was the master of the original Brutus." She said it loudly and defiantly. "Now. Let me introduce you to—"

Nellie Jean had no time to finish her sentence, for at that moment, the figure of a tall attractive man filled the doorway. He could be no one else but Russell MacGuire. His pioneer costume was nothing like the others; his pants fit tightly over his hips, the shirt was open, revealing a tanned hairy chest, and he wore no hat to cover his light, carefully combed hair.

Dana thought. *Here's a man who puts vanity above authenticity. He's making sure he looks great for the lead in the play.*

From that moment, she had no doubt he would take a different view of her calendars than did his cousin-with-the-attitude. Luckily the man was well built and had a sparkle in his dark eyes. He looked fine in the imaginary camera lens through which she viewed all young men.

The mayor of Devil's Fork stared at the woman in the pale green summer sundress with eyelet lace trim at her neck. Then he smiled. Charmer—the word she had heard at least three times in Marylee's Beauty Shop— described him, all right. His smile lit up the room.

"Dana French, isn't it?" He held out his hand. "Russ MacGuire. I want to offer my condolences on the loss of your great-aunt. Maude O'Connor was a beloved member of our community, and she will be missed by all of us."

Dana did not return his smile. "I had an appointment with you, but I see your office is pretty busy at the moment."

He frowned at his secretary. "Uh-oh. When I asked to have all my appointments canceled for the Players, I didn't realize one was with you. I wouldn't for the world inconvenience you."

Nellie Jean scowled back at him. The waiting actors were showing signs of restlessness. The children were banging sticks on a copper spittoon and trying to get the attention of the dog, who was licking the Indian's bare foot.

Dana tried her best to ignore all this. "I came," she said, "to find out why you want my house."

He glanced at the others, then studied the woman challenging him. His voice was soft. "I don't. I want the land."

"For any particular reason?"

He rubbed his chin and answered mildly, "Because I can get it cheap. You won't find another buyer."

Aware that he didn't appreciate her pursuing this in a room full of people, Dana determined to assert her right to be here. He had not canceled her appointment. "I don't want a buyer, Mr. MacGuire. I want to pay the taxes in installments. But I understand you are holding a lien—"

He interrupted. "Jake talked to you, did he?" This with a certain resentment, as if he thought Jake had no right to tell her what was obviously not public knowledge. "Tell you what, Miss French. You're welcome to stay and watch the rehearsal of our play. You might enjoy it. Afterward, we'll sit down and talk privately."

Dana met his eyes, which, unlike his voice, were uncompromising. This was not a berryderry sort of man. She accepted his suggestion unresentfully. He had, after all, agreed to talk to her. "I'd like to see the play," she said.

"Good." He began directing the costumed players. "Just a run-through," he announced. "Obviously we can't do as well without the real wagons. Tomorrow we'll work outside. For now I just want to see if Brutus-Spike is going to work out, or if we have to find another Brutus."

At the sound of his name, the boxer's ears went up. He trotted toward Russell curiously. Dana retreated to a far corner and sat down.

The players knew the script well. They had performed the play, she discovered, hundreds of times. Now and then someone new would take over one of the parts, but the characters were as familiar to the people of Devil's Fork as their contemporaries. The chairs in the room became three wagons. Russell and the dog occupied the first, Nellie Jean and her "wife" and three kids, the second, and the remaining couple the third.

Dana had some difficulty following the action. The first wagon was overturned by a flooded stream, and mayor and dog went crashing to the ground, where they were dragged through make-believe river mud with much gesturing and shouting from those in the wagons behind. On the sidelines stood the bandit and the Indian, slapping each other on the back, laughing like hyenas to see the pioneers wallowing in mud.

Then came the horror of the drama, as the masked bandit and his renegade Indian cohort named Sitting Duck began to steal supplies and livestock from the wagons.

"When we do it for real, we have real pigs and chickens," one of the children whispered as he ran past Dana trying to save a make-believe piglet from the bandit's clutches.

Brutus-Spike, who did not like being stolen by a painted man in feathers, growled and let out a resounding yap, which caused one of the pioneer women to scream. The mayor, pioneer Penrose MacGuire, was still flailing in the make-believe river.

Because the carefully reconstructed chaos seemed so deadly serious to the Players, Dana struggled for composure amid the squealing of imaginary pigs and the cackling of imaginary chickens and the shouting of the first settlers of Devil's Fork. She wondered what all this chaos had to do with the founding of the town.

A lull came over the room. Penrose MacGuire struggled out of the mud, clothes in disarray. Pioneers formed a pitiful circle to discuss their plight in well-rehearsed lines.

"We were warned about this fork in the trail."

"Devil's Fork is sure the name for it, all right."

Hands were raised in despair. "How can we go on?"

"We were told to look for a sign to tell us where to settle," Penrose MacGuire declared. "And we shall. We shall mend the wagon and go on, even without our animals."

After more minutes of wailed laments, there was a stir at the far end of the room where one of the children was holding Brutus-Spike. "Is it time?" the boy called.

"Don't ask if it's time," a woman answered. "When you get the signal for Brutus's entrance, just let him go."

"I'm trying. He's not going anywhere." The child pushed at the dog, who looked from one actor to the other with disdain.

"Brutus, it's your moment!" Nellie Jean coaxed from the pioneer circle. And to Russell, "What a dumb dog. He just stands there looking stupid. He's supposed to *bound*. You said he could bound."

"He can. He's a good bounder." Russell smacked his lips and snapped his fingers to coax the boxer nearer. The dog walked nonchalantly, pausing to sniff at the leg of an overturned "wagon."

"Look! It's Brutus bounding over the plain!" a pioneer shouted. "He got away from the Indian and he has come back!"

"Brutus has come back to us!" three others cried in unison.

The hero, Brutus, finally got there. He licked Nellie Jean's face, and she sputtered in protest.

"Look, he is digging in the mud!" a woman exclaimed.

Penrose MacGuire slipped a dog biscuit under a pillow. The dog sniffed it with interest. "Yes! He is digging!"

"But look!" shouted Nellie Jean, rising excitedly. "There is a gold nugget here in the mud! Brutus has found gold!"

"Our sign! Here we will stay to build our homes!"

"Here at Devil's Fork!"

"With gold washing down from the mountains!"

"Gold at Devil's Fork!"

"Hail, Brutus!"

"Hail, Brutus, brave and fine, / Escaped from the Indians and found our sign!"

"Man's best friend forever!"

The boxer, having nosed the pillow aside, sat down to enjoy the gold-nugget-biscuit. He was chomping loudly. Dana was suffering stomach pains from trying to hold back laughter. She was relieved when at last the Players began to disperse, talking animatedly about the less-than-enthusiastic performance of the hero dog. Nellie Jean took off the sweat-stained hat and shook down her hair.

Dana said, "I didn't realize gold had been discovered here."

Nellie Jean laughed. "Fool's gold. Oh, a minute amount of the real stuff washed down the river, but mostly it was fool's gold for the fools that settled at a fork where bandits hung out. Because of a dog. Now they fight over whose dog gets to play the lead in the play."

The room cleared after a few shooing gestures from Nellie Jean. Her boss approached, smoothing his light hair. "Schrock, for the outside rehearsal tomorrow, we need a photographer. I don't want to use the old photos of a different dog."

"I'll bring my camera," his secretary volunteered.

"I said photographer. I want great publicity shots."

"What am I, a magician? We don't have a photographer."

"Then try Eversville."

Dana squinted. Was she being set up? There was no way they could know they were standing beside a professional photographer unless Jake had told them.

"I'll see what I can do," Nellie Jean said.

When she left, Dana found herself standing face-to-face with the mayor of Devil's Fork, who was waiting expectantly for her to say something complimentary about the silliest performance she had ever witnessed. What she wanted to say was, "This is the weirdest town in the Western hemisphere." Instead, she smiled and said, "I can see why dogs are so important in Devil's Fork."

He smiled back. "It isn't every town that has a dog among its founders. We're proud of that."

"So I see. Such an impressive statue in the square."

The man's dark eyes were sparkling. "You saw only a rough rehearsal, Brutus-Spike's first try. We'll do better tomorrow."

"When you get photographs?"

He sighed. "Hopefully."

She looked at him levelly. "There *is* a professional photographer in town. You happen to be looking at her."

The way his face lit up, she knew Jake hadn't told him. Dana sat down on one of the few remaining upright chairs. "What I want is to keep my property and take care of the tax debt as I can. My credit is good. Are you agreed?"

The man rolled up the sleeve of his wrinkled pioneer-style shirt. "I'm afraid not. The city has debts, too."

Experience in approaching men for calendar layouts told Dana he was more conceited—and therefore more approachable—than his cousin. She straightened in the chair, aware that the bodice of her dress moved when she took a deep breath. "Well," she said, in her sweetest Texas drawl, "the truth is I'm grateful anyone would want to buy that awful old house. I've been hearing rumors that it's haunted, so goodness knows, maybe it truly is."

The mayor rested his elbows on his desk and made a tent with his fingers. "You want to own a haunted house?"

"Why not? There might be some sort of profit in it."

MacGuire laughed. "If it's really haunted."

"People here seem to think so, don't they? Are you one of them? Are you afraid of my aunt's house, Mayor?"

He laughed again and there was genuine amusement in his eyes. "I assure you I am not afraid of an old house, Dana. I hope I can call you Dana. Why are you looking at me like that?"

She pretended to be shocked. "Oh, was I staring? How dreadfully rude of me. It's a hazard of my profession, I'm afraid. I mentioned I'm a photographer. Actually, I specialize in photographing men, and I was— forgive me—picturing you as one of my artworks."

The man behind the desk squared his shoulders, smoothed his hair again and pushed the shirt higher on his arms to expose his elbows. "You photograph men?"

Dana laughed flirtatiously, feeling like a fool because such behavior betrayed everything she stood for. But the ghosts had to have their house. Thinking of her lady guests, she reached into her tote for a calendar. She handed it across to him, and sat forward, watching him flip through the months. January's ski instructor. February's construction worker. March's computer man with his sleeves rolled up. April's motorcycle cop.

The mayor of Devil's Fork looked at her quizzically. His biceps tightened noticeably. "Calendar men?"

"Real men," she said with a purr. "Not models. These guys are real and the art is real. I've won awards for some of these black-and-white photos. American men at work. I was staring because I was thinking how photogenic you are and how terrific to find a *mayor* who is calendar material! I would very much like the opportunity to photograph you. Oh, do say you'll agree. The photos will be respectable, I assure you. And you would receive a percentage of the proceeds. Think of the publicity for Devil's Fork!"

Russell's eyes shone with the flattery. Glancing through the rest of the calendar, he asked, "You think I'm—"

"Of course. You're very photogenic, and you know it."

The great thing was, this guy really was calendar material. Should she photograph him behind a podium? Throwing the first ball for a game? Leading a parade? She would emphasize his hands. He had good hands.

"It's a flattering offer, Dana," he was saying. "Politicians are gluttons for publicity."

And some men are gluttons for flattery, she thought, There was something about the mayor of Devil's Fork she instinctively disliked, a certain hardness about him. He was mean as a child, Inez had said. The so-called sinister sheriff might respond to the memory of a lullaby. Not the charming mayor. Maybe he wasn't a pushover, but even if this flattery didn't work, it wouldn't be wasted time; a town mayor would be great for September. She'd considered not bringing her camera on this trip, but experience had taught her that one could find subjects anywhere, so she'd set it in the front seat of her car. Thank heaven.

"Then you'll do it?" she asked.

"Sure, why not? Maybe we can work a deal. We need photographs of Brutus-Spike and the Town Players."

"Fine. What time is the rehearsal tomorrow? And what's your schedule like?"

"I'm giving a talk on fire safety at the high school tomorrow, and I have to appear in court for a hearing on property zoning. The rehearsal is at three in back of the courthouse. We keep the wagons on display there."

"Okay. I'll work with your schedule over the next two days. I'll take actual job shots, but they must be sexy. You understand."

He was looking at her in a way she did not like; she'd encountered that look before. This shoot was going to have to be handled carefully, but Dana wasn't worried about being able to take care of herself; she'd been in this business long enough.

His chest expanded. "Sexy, huh? Sounds like a challenge."

She forced a smile. "With the right subject the sexuality is already there. All I have to do is give it emphasis with the camera." Uncomfortable with him and wanting to leave, she stood up. "Wear a shirt that isn't white. White doesn't photograph well. I'll get your schedule from Nellie Jean, and take some shots of you in action, and we'll see what we get."

He rose. "Are you in a hurry?"

"Yes," she lied. "I have a million things to do at the house. I'm taking inventory." She backed away. She wanted desperately to ask him to reconsider the situation with the house, but the timing wasn't right. Better to wait until he saw his photos and was impressed with how great she'd made him look. She would get him fantasizing about having his photos on a nationally distributed calendar—*if* she chose his. Then she'd have bargaining power.

Dana left his office feeling as if she'd been in that make-believe mud. She didn't like Russell MacGuire's kind of conceit, and she didn't like the way he looked at her. If only she could just walk away from the madness of this town, but life wasn't that simple. She was the ghosts' only hope for saving their house. And she *was* going to save it!

In the outer office, Nellie Jean, now wearing a crisp blouse and skirt, was working at her desk. "You must have come about Russell's lien on your house. I saw the file just yesterday when Jake asked for it. Is Russ going to take the property off your hands, then?"

"Not if I can help it. I want the house. But Russell seems to want it, too."

Nellie Jean pursed her thin lips. "That's interesting."

Dana began to feel some of her tension release. Nellie Jean Schrock was genuine, and therefore calming. "I'm going to take the pictures of the Players tomorrow, and some of the mayor, but I need a darkroom for developing my prints. Any chance of finding one?"

"An acquaintance of mine in Eversville does some photography for the county paper. We could try her."

"Great. I want to get Russell's schedule. I'm going to photograph him for a calendar layout."

The woman's eyes grew wide. "What?"

Dana laughed. "Not the kind you think. Although—" she leaned forward "—I'm tempted—I truly am . . ."

Nellie Jean broke into laughter. "Our mayor on a calendar? That ought to get Devil's Fork noticed! What are you up to, Dana? Might this have something to do with the property lien?"

Dana laughed. "Such wicked thoughts you have."

"Hell's bells. Don't I know all there is to know about getting around the conceited macho twosome running this town? Did you give up trying to get the sheriff's help?"

"Not yet."

"Jake is harder to manipulate than Russell, because Russell is more concerned about his public image." Nellie Jean glanced toward the closed door of the mayor's office. "Why do you want the house? I mean, in my opinion, it's a fabulous old place, but its run-down, and it's not as if you live there."

"I don't want to see it torn down."

"I'll help any way I can. Maybe I can find out why Russ wants it, other than the fact he can get it for a song. Even if he leased the meadow for pasture, there'd be little profit." She glanced at the door again. "Dana, I just heard that your great-aunt Maude had a secret lover for twenty or thirty years—someone prominent in town. The whole place is buzzing about it! They say you told Marylee at the Beauty Shop."

Dana grinned. "Incredibly, I started the rumor barely an hour ago."

"You mean it's *true?*"

"No. I just wanted to start a rumor."

Nellie Jean doubled over, unable to keep her laughter controlled. "But why?"

"Because I wanted to get into the circle of gossip over there. To find out more about the people of Devil's Fork, particularly the mayor."

The woman behind the desk grabbed a tissue to wipe her eyes. "Your dear aunt—oh, she would have loved it!"

Dana studied her. Not everyone would have recognized Maude's mischievous side. Nellie Jean must have understood her. "Yes, Maude would have loved it."

"Dana, why are you confiding this to me?"

"I have a sixth sense about people. I believe you and I think alike, and I could use a friend in this town." *And almost everybody else I've encountered is ready for the loony bin,* she thought.

The other woman smiled warmly. "It's not such a bad town when you get used to it." Looking at the clock on the wall, she said, "It's nearly lunchtime. Do you want to have a bite to eat with me?"

"Sure. If we can go someplace where Russell won't see me and realize I lied about having to rush home."

"No problem. There's a sandwich shop around the corner. Chef Lou's. I'll meet you there in ten minutes."

A bond was forming between them. It was comforting to Dana to know she had an ally.

8

JAKE WAS CURRYING his dogs on the porch steps, but his mind wasn't on his task. When he'd left Dana he'd felt that something wasn't quite right. He hadn't been able to shake the feeling; it had stayed with him, clinging like a damp mist all the next day.

Who was she? Why did she stir such unfamiliar feelings in him? How did she know things about his past that no one could know unless she had some extraordinary psychic powers? He had never believed in that sort of thing, yet he could come up with no other answer to his hundreds of questions—questions that all came down to one question: *Who was she?*

She made him remember gentler, softer days—snowflakes on the windows and dew-wet lilacs on spring mornings. She made him remember what it was like to savor being alive and drink in joy with the sunshine and dance around rain puddles. She made him sad, because she was a reminder of how sterile his life had become. How many sunsets had he watched these past years without feeling their beauty because his heart was too frozen to see the magic in the colors?

How many women had walked in front of him and he hadn't even looked? He was looking now. Trying not to think of Dana was like trying to ignore a persistent pain. Yet when he thought of her, it was excitement, not pain, that raced through his veins. He had to see her again. To learn more about her. To drink in the aroma of her perfume. To wonder at her beauty.

Jake was trying to work up an excuse to drive to the O'Connor house when Russell's car appeared in his drive. He continued to comb the white terrier while his cousin got out of the car and joined him. Twice in one week Russ had come out; again there was some reason, Jake was sure.

"What's new?" he asked, barely looking up.

Russ was wearing jeans and a dark T-shirt. "You got a cold beer? It's been quite a day."

"Help yourself."

Moments later Jake heard the screen door squeak behind him and Russell emerged from the house carrying a can of beer. Jake heard the screen door squeak behind him.

Jake said, "You have an obnoxious grin on your face. What are you grinning about?"

"I've been posing for photos all day. Fascinating experience, working with a real pro."

Instantly Jake saw red. His reaction surprised him, but he couldn't deny his angry reaction. He tried to keep his voice even. "That would be Dana French, I assume."

"You assume right. She took one look at me and wanted to photograph me for a calendar."

Jake brushed harder at the dog's flanks. "That ought to do wonders for your image."

Russell laughed loudly. "Clothed, my man, fully clothed, but as Dana put it, 'showing the muscles and the well-placed veins.'" He laughed again at Jake's sullen silence. "I saw the woman's work. Real art. She knows what she's doing, and she knows a photogenic male when she sees one."

Jake's anger grew hotter. Dana had asked him to pose and he had turned her down. Now she was manipulating Russell and it was working. Russ was grinning like a goose.

Jealousy. He was seething with jealousy. Jake gritted his teeth. *She asked me first,* the child in him taunted, but he would not say it and give Russ the satisfaction of knowing he cared. Russell was the opportunist. Jake had blown it.

"Well?" His cousin prodded him. "What do you think of having a relative whose photo is soon to be gazed at longingly by thousands of American women? It'll put old Devil's Fork on the map, that's for sure. This ought to settle the matter once and for all over which of us is more irresistible to the opposite sex."

Jake could have told him why Dana was doing this, but he wouldn't. He himself had been won over by her mysterious charm. "Are you going to cancel the lien as a gesture of goodwill after she's done you the honor of photographing you?"

Russell gazed at him. "No, why should I?"

"Because you have no use for the house and she wants it."

"It's business. Come to your senses, Cuz! One doesn't mix business with one's modeling career. If you had more of a business sense you'd be as well-off as I am. You could have held on to your share of the business."

Jake scowled. "I never liked being business partners with you. I had to watch my back every minute."

The mayor set his beer can on the step. "Are you saying I would cheat you?"

"Anytime you got a chance."

"Well, now, I resent that. Just because I'm always looking for deals and loopholes—"

"I like operating above the table." Jake pulled dog hair off the currycomb. "That's a stale topic, anyhow. We're better off not being partners—we're both happier in our own pastures, so let's drop it." Patting the dogs, he sent them on their way. "Go chase meadow rabbits," he suggested, but all three canines chose instead to socialize on the porch.

Jake stood up and stretched. "I don't mean to be inhospitable, glamor boy, but I have plans for tonight."

"What plans?" Russell asked suspiciously. This was a tactical error, for neither had questioned the other about his personal plans since they were in junior high.

So, Jake thought, *he's worried I might have an interest in Dana.* That meant Russ had an interest in her, too, but this was no surprise. Russ went for all beautiful women.

Jake answered, "My plans are my business."

He wanted to go in and shower and clean up, but Russell was alerted. If he delayed getting over to the O'Connor house, he could expect Russell to be there first.

Russell stood up. "Dana is photographing me again tomorrow, at the courthouse. All those pictures and she'll choose only one for her calendar. She says I'm September."

Feeling in his pocket for the keys to his pickup, Jake began to walk toward the drive. Russell followed reluctantly, the three dogs at his heels.

"What's your hurry?"

"I'm late."

"For what?"

Jake answered sarcastically, "For getting in the ice-cream-cone line at Smiling Sadie's Dairy Barn, what else?"

"All right, don't get smart." Russ patted the head of the bloodhound. "You're just jealous because she asked me to pose, instead of you."

"She did ask me."

"Sure she did! Sure! Next you'll be claiming one of these dogs was in the running to play Brutus."

"Believe what you want. You always do." Jake got into his truck and opened the window. "Have fun tomorrow. Don't let your eye shadow run. Oh, and don't wear a red tie. Red makes you look wimpy."

"You're not taking this well." Russell grinned as he turned toward his own car.

Jake pulled out of the driveway fast, then, as soon as his cousin's sleek car was out of sight, slowed to a crawl. He was headed for the O'Connor house, unexpected and unannounced, which meant it would be difficult to try to pass off the visit as business. Anyway, why try? Maybe Dana knew he would show up.

Damn. She was photographing Russell, spending two days with him, planning to con him into giving her time to pay the taxes. Jake drove fast and then slow and then fast again, working on an excuse for showing up at her door.

For the first time in his life he was jealous of his cousin, and the feeling sat very badly with him. As he drove, it began to dawn on Jake that he had not experienced such emotions in a great many years. He thought of the blueberryderries. He thought of the way small shadows spun in the silk of her blouse when she moved.

And he thought about Russell's obnoxious grin, and gritted his teeth. Russell would play this one for all he was worth unless Jake moved in first.

She mattered to him. Dana French had begun to occupy his mind, and he did not object. To his surprise, he welcomed the mystery of her.

DANA FINISHED watering Maude's many plants in the glassed-in side porch. She sat down to drink her tea in the company of her six unusual boarders. "In the mayor's office I watched the Town Players rehearse their play about the founding of Devil's Fork."

Rosella cackled. "Rehearse? How many times can those fools go over one play?"

"They had a new member of the cast. A boxer named Brutus-Spike. The rehearsal was for Brutus-Spike's benefit."

"A boxer now, is it?" Inez said with such disgust Dana was startled.

Dana smiled. "I was surprised at that, too, I mean since the Brutus statue in the square looks nothing like Brutus-Spike. I was told no one knows what breed Brutus actually was."

"The Town Players are such cabbage heads," Rosella scoffed.

Louise piped up with, "When I had the part of Marsha—that's one of the pioneer women—I made that role really *live*. I knew how to play it authentically. We had a beautiful Labrador retriever as Brutus in those days."

Inez raised one hand. "We don't want to talk about Brutus, girls, do we? That has been our pact. No talk about Brutus."

Dana looked from one to the other, shaking her head. There was no point in trying to make sense of Devil's Fork's ridiculous history. What was the big deal about the dog?

"You've barely touched on the Beauty Shop report," Frances reminded her.

Dana set down her teacup. "A woman named Greta came into the shop just before I left—a blond woman with a long thick braid. She said Neil and Edna Maxwell are getting a divorce because Edna has been having an affair with the vet who delivered their twin calves."

This bit of news brought gasps all around.

"Edna didn't love Neil in the first place," Rosella said. "She was pregnant when they got married."

"She was not!" Louise brushed back a lock of wispy hair. "That was mean gossip and not true."

"It was true," argued Rosella. "Maude heard it at the bridal shower. She was pregnant by Bernard Sharpy. Even Neil didn't know."

"I hope not." Dana grinned. She blew on the hot tea. "Didn't I see this story on a soap opera once?"

Louise pipped up again with, "That Greta is a fine one to spread tales. She held rich old Mrs. Drew captive in her house, waiting for the poor old thing to change her will. And just because Greta wanted Mrs. Drew's antique one-horse open sleigh."

Dana sighed, feeling drained. It was all too much to absorb, including her joy at being with the ladies of the club. Not for a long time had she laughed so much.

"Tell me about your grandson Russell," she said to Inez, thinking about today's photo session.

The ghost smiled with fond memories. "I mentioned that Russ and Jake used to get into trouble rather a lot as children. When they got in hot water, Russell's father, my son James, tended to make excuses for his son and get him out of the mess. My Johnny, Jake's father, took an opposite approach and made Jake take the consequences of his actions. Because of that, most people thought Jake was the wilder of the two boys, but he wasn't, he was just less sneaky. Why do you ask, my dear?"

Dana sipped her tea slowly, trying not to show the nervousness she felt about the ghosts' problem. "Russell wants the land here, including the land under this house," she said. "I don't think he can be swayed. I haven't given up hope, of course. Certainly he'll be impressed when he sees his photos."

Dana felt at ease with the ghosts. She had a connection with them she hadn't had with living people, the sort of interdependence and common commitment that families have. She had missed having a family. After her parents died, she'd lived with her mother's sister Eve, who was kind, but not like a mother. Her cousin Sam, five years younger, had resented Dana's moving into his house. Eve and Sam had never felt like real family. Maude had been a distant figure in her life—Dana had seen her so seldom—but she always felt love coming from her, and Dana had loved her back. Now she had this unique and marvelous chance to get to know her. As the ghosts' dependence on her grew, the more she cared about them.

Looking at them now, gathered around while she drank her tea, Dana could barely hold back tears. This strange circle of kindly souls was the family she never had, and just when she was getting to know them, she would lose them because she didn't know how to keep their house.

"Is something the matter?" Frances asked.

Dana quickly wiped her eyes. "I just feel so helpless."

"You are far from helpless. Look at all you've been doing, baking and cooking and taking pictures of the mayor."

The doorbell chimed. Dana gave a start. "I'm not expecting anyone."

She removed the antique eyeglasses as she made her way through the house. When she opened the front door, Jake MacGuire stood in the long summer shadows of the giant maple trees. Behind him the sky was pale with twilight, and a half-moon was beginning to show itself high in the sky.

For some moments neither spoke. "Hi," Dana said finally, and opened the door wider.

"Hi." Jake did not step in. Instead, he scratched the back of his neck self-consciously and said, because it was the first thing that popped into his head, "Would you be interested in helping with a police investigation?"

This was a surprise. "Who, me? A stranger in town?"

"That's the point. You're the only person who would be an objective observer and not a suspect."

Dana wasn't sure what was going on. Was this an odd attempt to establish a friendship, or was he really involved in a criminal investigation that required an outsider's help? And did he mean that everyone in the entire town was on his list of possible suspects?

"It's nothing dangerous," he hastened to add.

"What sort of crime are you talking about?"

"Theft. Break-and-enter and theft."

Dana felt a rush of adrenaline. The air between them was so alive with excitement she expected it to crackle.

"Do you want to come in and tell me about it?"

Jake scuffed his boot on the weathered porch floor. "It's a nice evening. There's a concert down at the river, if you like the sound of frogs and locusts and a bob-white or two. Would you like to walk by the river with me?"

Was this for real? His visit was about more than enlisting her help. Something had changed. No, everything had changed. During the day with Russell, she hadn't been able to stop thinking about Jake. Had he been thinking all day of her, too? Was it possible? Her heart began beating harder. He wanted to walk in the twilight with her! Or was it just that he didn't feel comfortable in the old house?

"I'd like to very much," she answered, reaching back to close the door behind her.

He took her hand and led her down the porch steps and out onto the meadow. The river lay beyond a line of thick tall trees at the far side of the stretch of green meadow. Jasmine perfumed the air. Birds sang in the shadows of branches overhead.

She felt his nearness as they walked through the flower-studded grass. His hand was radiating heat in her own. If he held on too long, flames might ignite— could he feel that heat, too? Dana waited for more information about his criminal investigation, and when it didn't come, she asked, "What do you want me to do?"

He looked at her. "What?"

"To help you catch this thief? Did you want to set a trap in my house or something?"

"Where I could use your help," he said hesitantly, "is at the supermarket. Observing people around the meat counter and reporting any suspicious behavior. If I try it, no one will act normally."

Dana stared at him. *I'm in Nutsville, USA, and I've known it since I got here.* "The meat counter. Sure. You're sure this under-cover assignment isn't dangerous, now?"

Jake laughed. "I thought maybe you'd have heard about the crime spree we've been having. Someone has been walking into houses and stealing hams from refrigerators. A few days ago the person didn't walk in, he broke in. Whoever it is checks out the market to see who is buying hams, I'm sure of it."

She studied him suspiciously. "Jake, are you serious?"

"Absolutely. People are getting real upset. I tried putting indelible dye on one ham—in cooperation with the buyer, of course. If a thief tries to wash the dye off, it gets worse. The idea was to see if anyone showed up anywhere with blue hands."

"And they didn't?"

He blanched. "No. What happened was Millie Stanfors's mother—Millie was the one helping me with the trap—her mother got into the ham, instead, and the dye was all over her hands and face. She was unable to attend a funeral that was the social event of the month. I had to take her four gallons of strawberries to make up for it."

"I see." Dana tried not to smile because Jake was not smiling. "Well, I'm good at reading people. If anyone could spot a suspect stalking the meat counter, it'd be me."

Jake slowed his pace. "It might be more difficult than it sounds because the market is a general meeting place. A lot of people are there just standing around and talking."

"I'm good at body language. I have a trained eye."

"Then you'll do it?"

"Sure."

"Good. Thanks." He released her hand and bent down to pick a small handful of pale pink flowers, which he handed to her. "When I was a kid we called these pink snowflakes. I've always thought they were the most beautiful thing in the valley. Then I met you."

The delicate flowers trembled in Dana's hand. She lifted the petals to her cheek and felt their softness. The perfume was like the smell of a gentle wind moving through grass. "Mmm. Pink snowflakes." She smiled up at him. "Thanks for the compliment."

"Less compliment than fact."

"Why did you leave so abruptly last night?" she asked.

"Certain things you say bother me because you seem able to see into my life. Who are you, Dana? To walk into my world like you've been here before, as if you already know me. Did you know me once and I don't remember?"

I've been shamefully unfair to him, she thought. *I've not been playing fair.* But she couldn't confess; the ghosts had not given their consent for her to do that. Besides, who'd believe she was in a conspiracy with ghosts?

She shook her head. "I didn't already know you. How could I?"

"Who are you, Dana?"

"Just a photographer from Dallas."

Jake had not taken her hand again, but he walked close as they neared the dark shadows of the river. "Russell told me you're photographing him for your calendar."

"Yes. For September."

"Not July?"

"You would have been July, Jake, only you wouldn't do it."

"You were trying to bribe me to get me to cooperate about the house. Russell, being a politician, is easier to bribe."

"You make me sound awful."

"You're not awful, you're determined, and using what resources are available to you. I admire you for that."

"You didn't seem to admire it when I suggested you pose for me. And the truth is, I'd have asked you under any circumstances. You are exactly the type I look for. I consider myself a treasure hunter. Now and then I discover a treasure. My calendars are so successful because I have a good eye."

"And Russell?"

Dana wouldn't lie to him. "I might not have asked Russell if I weren't trying to get on his good side. Although, I think he might work. He's handsome and not your typical mayor."

A sound like a low growl came from Jake's throat. "What's the difference between September and July?"

Aha! Dana thought. *Rivalry here!*

"It should be obvious, Jake. July is the hottest month."

She could have sworn he flushed. His pace slowed. If her instincts were right, he was not the least bit pleased that his cousin might be September. "You could change your mind, you know," she offered demurely.

"Well, I might."

"You don't want Russell to get the better of you, huh?"

"I don't want you taking his picture and not mine. I look better."

"Yes," she agreed. "You do." *In those tight jeans and that short-sleeved shirt, you sure do.*

It was too bad, she thought, that the camera could not capture the reflection of blue shirt in his sky-blue eyes.

The compliment appeased him. He said, "I feel I ought to warn you about my cousin. He'll make a play for you. Russ is not always an honorable mayor."

"And you want to protect me? From him?"

"As a matter of fact, I do."

The fluting and croaking of the frogs grew louder as they neared the riverbank. Jake took a deep breath. "When it hit me that Russell would make a move, I got the hell over here, Dana. I needed to know how you felt."

"About what?"

"About me. About walking with me on a summer night."

The magic of the evening was like soft fluttering butterfly wings. Dana found herself savoring the nearness of him, knowing these moments would never leave her memory.

"I'm sure you knew I'd love to walk with you on the meadow, or you wouldn't have asked."

His shoulders relaxed. "I couldn't be that sure. I've never met a woman like you."

"I've never met a man like you, either."

"Is that good?"

"I think so."

They were in the shadows of the giant cottonwoods that grew along the riverbanks. The twilight was soft and pink; there was a hush and then the frogs began to sing. Jake paused, looked at her for a long, searching moment, then took her into his arms. His lips moved toward hers slowly, and when she raised her head toward him his warm mouth cornered hers.

Dana closed her eyes and floated on sensations that soared beyond anything she had ever known.

In the blur of pleasure, she had a sense of being entrusted with a great secret. In spite of the rumors, in spite of his cold exterior, Jake MacGuire was not untouchable.

Quite the contrary. The blood in his veins flowed as hot as that of any other man. If the rumors were true, few women had felt the heat of his touch or known the passion of his kiss.

He moved his fingers through her hair and smoothed the loose strands around her face. "I'm very attracted to you."

She let the weight of her body blend into his so that it was his strength holding her up.

"Is the attraction mutual, Dana?"

"Yes . . ."

When he kissed her again, the questions of the first touch had been answered and only passion remained.

His need was powerful and she felt it, reeled under the force of it. It caught and held her captive.

"I don't know who you are," Jake said huskily, "but I think I love you."

9

DANA GASPED, head spinning, legs numb. His arms around her were an invincible force, and within them she felt no danger, only safety.

She whispered, "These feelings I have—I don't know what they are."

"But they're strong."

"Yes."

"For me."

She nodded against his chest. They stood listening to nature's concert while he kissed her forehead and her hair. "It's impossible, though, Jake. I live so far away. I can't stay in Devil's Fork long enough to . . . to love you."

He gazed down at her with the sunset reflecting in his eyes. "You're here now."

"Yes, but—"

"Then there is only tonight to think about," he said. "This is a night that will never be again."

"What are you talking about—this night? It's too soon to talk about . . . love, isn't it?"

His eyes had a faraway look. "There isn't some magical time frame that comes with love. It just happens." He touched her lips with his fingertips. "Dana, I don't love easily or often."

"I know. I've heard about you."

Jake cocked his head to one side. "What have you heard?"

"That many women have their eyes on you and you don't respond to any of them. That you are made of steel."

"I'm as prone to loneliness as any other man. But choosier than most when it comes to women. Like I said, I don't love easily, but I feel a strong attraction to you. And I want you."

Her voice trembled. "Which is it? Love or attraction?"

"Both."

"But how can you know you love me?"

"I know what I feel and I know what I want. A year from tonight I might love you more than I do this minute, but I won't love you less." Jake frowned then, studying her. "Is there another man in your life?"

"No, no other man. Not now."

"But there has been?"

"Once or twice, but . . ." Her voice trailed off.

"But not the right man."

Dana shivered. Jake's magnetism was drawing her in. The newness of him, the secret of him! The smell of his skin, the fire of his touch. No man had ever affected her this way.

His hand caressed her shoulder. She yielded to still another of his seducing kisses while the magic butterflies darted and dived through her stomach.

At length she pulled away. "I can't do this, Jake. It's too crazy . . ."

He held her chin gently. "Because you think it's too soon?"

"Yes. Too fast . . ."

"I understand."

This was not the response Dana expected. She had been prepared to have to plead for his kisses to stop.

"You do? You understand why I can't . . ."

"Of course. I told you I want you, but you have to want me. You have to feel right about it."

"I feel confused. This is so temporary, Jake."

He was caressing her cheek with one finger, softly. "Will you feel differently a week from now?"

"A week from now I might not even be here."

"I hope to God you are."

He had allowed her to draw away. He took her hand and led her along the bank, breathing deeply of the evening air.

"You overwhelm me, Jake."

He didn't smile. "I am the one overwhelmed. You've made me remember feelings I'd forgotten I had, and I don't know if that's good or bad, considering what you keep pointing out—that you don't belong in Devil's Fork."

Her body tingled mercilessly. *I can't fall in love with him. I can't be in love with him. I can't be. I can't want him. But I do. As wildly as he seems to want me.*

"It's okay," he said gently. "I know it was too soon to tell you how I feel about you. But I believe in saying what I feel—no games. You baffle me and you make me love you and, yes, I do know what love is and, yes, it can happen fast."

I think so, too, Dana thought, afraid to say it for fear of losing control of her emotions completely.

Jake slid his arm around her waist and they walked in silence along the bank. Ahead of them frogs leapt into the water making silvery splashes that set the reeds to swaying gently. Crickets were conversing in the grass, and from the trees came the cry of a curlew. "It will soon be dark," he said. "We'd better head back."

As they approached the house, Dana found herself in a dilemma. She did not want to ask him in because they wouldn't be alone, yet she couldn't explain why they wouldn't be alone.

She paused at the top of the steps. Jake leaned forward in the shadows of the tall maple tree and gave her a long and tender kiss. "It's okay," he whispered as if he'd read her mind. "I think you need time alone to absorb this. What about tomorrow night? Shall we have dinner together?"

"I'd like to."

"Good. I'll pick you up at six-thirty."

"Could you make it seven? After I finish shooting in the morning, I'm going to take the film over to Eversville and develop it there, and I don't know what time I'll get back."

"Seven's fine." He took her hand. "I'll be jealous of Russell tomorrow. Maybe I'll pose for you, after all."

She smiled. "I wish you would." If only she could see his eyes in the dark, get one more look at his eyes. "What about the ham-theft investigation? When do you need me?"

"We'll make a plan tomorrow. Good night, Dana."

"Good night."

He turned to go then turned back. "I'll do whatever I can to influence Russell to cooperate in your house situation. I can't promise anything, though. He's a stubborn man. I can't fathom why you want this old place, but if it keeps you in Devil's Fork, I don't care why."

Dana was reeling with love's miracle. She believed Jake's words; she had seen the love in his eyes. This was the real thing! Dazedly, she watched him cross the grassy lawn to his truck and waved at him as he got in.

For a long time she stood on the step, not hearing the curlew or the locusts; hearing only Jake's voice saying over and over, "I love you."

Now what do I do?

Allow herself these wild and tender feelings that were gripping her? She didn't dare! The thought of loving him was almost terrifying. There could be only heartbreak ahead, because she lived in Texas and he lived in Devil's Fork.

Inside, the presence of the ghosts was soft and sweet and welcoming. Because of them, it felt good to come home. Because of them, she had a family. And certainly a family secret.

She wouldn't confide in them about tonight, though. She didn't dare. The Ladies' Club was a gossip factory, and even though the information could go no further than this house, it would be made much of and discussed at great length. Dana wasn't ready for that. And it didn't seem fair to Jake.

So she did not put on the glasses as she went up to bed, barely feeling the steps under her feet. She still felt his kisses. His eyes still cast their spell. His voice still echoed words of love. Dana's heart was still beating at twice its normal rate. She swelled with happiness that a man like him could love her.

What of Devil's Fork? Was it a trap? Jake wanted her. The ghosts wanted her. The house wanted her. She didn't belong in this crazy town, but it seemed that even the town wanted her. It was spinning its web around her, holding her captive in soft easy ways, making her laugh and cry. Making her feel alive. Making her fall in love.

IT WAS ALMOST NOON. By ten o'clock Dana had photographed the mayor in the courthouse reading court documents, with light slanting down on his face from a high window. He wore a fine dark sports jacket and a smile on his face that she wanted to get away from as soon as possible. The whispered innuendos he had made before the shooting were suggestive and out of line. Russell thought it was charm. A few other people must think so, too, or they wouldn't have elected him to office.

Nellie Jean Schrock, who did not seem enamored of the mayor, was waiting for her outside the courtroom. Dana said, "I hate to trouble you about this."

"No trouble. Eversville is only twenty-eight miles away and I can use an afternoon off." Nellie Jean swung her handbag over her shoulder. "Come on. We'll take my car."

At the edge of town, they passed the velvet-green cemetery. Dana thought of Jake's wife, whose grave was probably there, and of the ghosts whose graves must be there, too.

Nellie Jean grinned as she drove. "That's my land you're looking at."

"The cemetery?"

"Yep. Been in my family for generations. It's a great income property."

"If you sell plots, how can you still own them?"

"I don't sell plots. My great-grandfather stipulated that his land can never be sold. So I lease plots. Long leases. I'm a landlord whose tenants are dead." She laughed. "At least there are no tenant complaints."

Dana shook her head. *Where else but in Devil's Fork?* She liked Nellie Jean Schrock. She was beginning to like Devil's Fork, too. In the midst of the eccentricity was a gentle reality she felt more every day. Innocence and kindness resided here. She said, "Your name came up at Marylee's Beauty Shop."

The woman laughed. "Doesn't it always? I'm a main gossip target. I keep them on their toes, I do."

"Why you, Nellie Jean?"

"Because I own half this town, and people can't figure out whether or not I ever intend to marry."

"I heard you linked romantically with the preacher."

"That's no rumor. Donald and I are a red-hot item."

"The clientele were debating heatedly whether or not you're going to marry him. Are you?"

"Only if he stays in Devil's Fork. Sometimes he talks of going to Nashville to become the next Kenny Rogers without the tumbleweed. If he does, I won't go."

"Do you love him?"

"Madly."

"Well, then, I don't understand. If it's true love . . ."

Nellie Jean pursed her lips thoughtfully. "True love is this town and me. Hell, Dana, sometimes I think I *am* this town." She paused. "I tell you this in confidence—someday I'm going to run this town."

Dana blinked. "You mean you want to be mayor?"

"Not want to be. I will be."

"Can Russell MacGuire be voted out of office?"

"Not now. He's as popular as a firecracker on the Fourth of July, but I'll find a way to get him out. Either he'll mess up one of his shady deals or somehow I'll find the secret."

"Are you saying Russ is underhanded?"

"In more ways than one. Take that lien on your property, for example. One of his ploys is to offer loans to people in need and get a lien. He's taken over two properties I know of that way, and tried to take over three more. Takes advantage of people's troubles. You watch him, Dana. He'll try to date you if he hasn't already, and women say he isn't one for casual dating, if you know what I mean."

"I've already been warned about him by the sheriff."

Nellie Jean's eyebrows shot up. "You've been talking a lot with the sheriff?"

"Well, he is the tax assessor and I have got a tax problem." *Whatever I say will spread all over town, especially if it is about Jake,* she thought, pulling back. She changed the subject as quickly as possible. "Nellie Jean, what did you mean, you'd find the secret of getting Russell out of office? You mean exposing his shady deals?"

"His deals are always inside the law, if just barely. No, I meant *the* secret. I'm convinced there's a deep dark secret buried somewhere in Devil's Fork. I think the ladies of the club knew that secret. It bound them together and enabled them to run this town—to always, and I mean always, get their way."

Dana straightened. "I've been under the impression they did it through gossip blackmail."

"Oh, they did. But there was something more. There had to be. That Ladies' Club was terrific, Dana. Those old gals knew how to run a town. I've admired them all my life. I've also suspected for a long time that they were blackmailing the town government with this deadly secret."

Dana scowled. "Blackmail is no better than Russell's dealings, is it?"

Nellie Jean looked at her in surprise. "There's a huge difference, Dana. What the club did was always for the good of the town. The interests of the citizens was all they cared about and if it took blackmail to keep a politician honest, they used it! No shady deals or lining of pockets in those days. Our present mayor, on the other hand, has only his own welfare in mind; he cheats people, works private deals for his own financial gain.

"It's a power thing. The ladies liked mischief but they had power because they spread love all over this town. I tried to talk to your great-aunt before she died, hoping she'd pass it on to me, but I could get nothing out of her. *That's* how ghastly that secret is!"

"Maybe there is no secret," Dana said weakly, wondering, *If there was, would they tell me?*

"There's a secret, all right. I'm positive."

A storm began to rage inside Dana. *What if this is true? What secret could be that deadly? Would they tell me if it meant saving their house?*

"I'll find out someday, some way," Nellie Jean was saying. "I'm a determined woman. This is my town and I don't like it run by a politician who cheats people when he can. What we need here is more love. Brutuslove, I call it. More people helping each other. The Ladies' Club knew that. They're probably up there running a whole wing of heaven right now."

They arrived in Eversville, a town more modern in appearance than Devil's Fork, and pulled up at a photography studio off the main street.

Devil's Fork needs a photography studio like this, Dana found herself thinking. The photographer, a stout, plain woman in her thirties, wheezed in surprise as she watched Dana's photos come to life in her darkroom. "It's Mayor MacGuire! Whoa, look at this! Your mayor is a handsome one, right enough, but I never knew he looked this good!"

Dana studied the photos as they came clear before her eyes. Russell did look good, better than in life, thanks to her expertise. The more she stared at the photos, the more his eyes disturbed her. Dishonest eyes? Did the camera bring that out, or was she influenced by what Nellie Jean had been telling her?

Driving back to Devil's Fork, Dana studied the photos. Yes, definitely, there was an expression in the eyes of September that was not attractive. Jake's photos would be very different, she thought dreamily, allowing thoughts of him to wash over her unchecked, now that the workday was over and it would not be long before she saw him again. Jake's eyes—the eyes of July—would be cool eyes, but honest. They had told her as clearly as his voice had told her that he was in love with her. Thinking about his declaration of love held her in a suspended state of euphoria.

"Do you want to come over for a plate of macaroni?" Nellie Jean asked. "I boil macaroni better than anybody else in the county—ask anyone. Have it every night with ketchup."

This brought Dana out of her reverie. From Jake's eyes to macaroni with ketchup was a jolt. "Uh, I already have plans."

The eyebrows shot up. "Aha! Which one of them is it? Surely not Jake. He never dates. Omigod! Russell has worked his grizzly charm on you?"

"Jake," she said cautiously.

"Well, I'll be a mossback dizzard! How in blazes did you cut through that wall of brambles? Huh?"

"I can't say," Dana replied. "Maybe he likes my cooking."

What a lie, Dana told herself, flushing. The way she wanted him, the way he wanted her... What lay in store tonight?

No! She had to be sane about this! The closer she allowed Jake to get to her, the more it would hurt when she left. Dana closed her eyes. The thought of leaving Devil's Fork and the ghosts and the man who loved her already hurt badly.

DANA FELT the high energy in the house the moment she stepped in the door. The ghosts were hovering. Good. She had questions for them.

She went into the kitchen where she kept the antique eyeglasses and put them on. The ghosts were all there, chattering, and the chatter was about Inez's two grandsons.

Rosella lifted herself weightlessly to the countertop, her favorite seat. "We've been going over the possibilities," she began. "Inez thinks it would be a good idea to make a polka-dot teddy bear for Jake to remind him of the bear he slept with every night as a child. Maude says a better plan is to carry on trying to break down Russell's defenses in case the calendar photos don't win him over."

Maude floated closer. "You could invite him here and serve peanut-butter-and-jelly milk shakes, which Inez said he relished as a boy."

Dana winced, then laughed. "Peanut-butter-and-jelly milk shakes? The macho mayor?"

"He invented them himself, as I recall," said Inez.

"Be that as it may, ladies, I don't think a milk shake is going to shake up that guy. I'm going to insinuate that the final decision about September's page isn't made yet. Let him try to influence me. I think he understands that kind of exchange. But I'm worried about it, because I think he has some reason for wanting this property that he isn't ready to divulge, something that even Jake doesn't know about."

"Then we must continue to concentrate on Jake," Inez said. "He is the only one who can influence Russell. I know Russell is afraid of him. We can continue to try to reach Jake's sentimental side."

Dana smiled at the old woman affectionately. Her heart went out to all of them; they were trying so hard to find ways of saving their house, and the ways were so . . . so silly. Yet, their silliness certainly had made an impression on the poor unsuspecting sheriff. "A polka-dot bear? It isn't necessary, Inez. Jake is won over already."

Maude moved around the table, passing in front of Frances. Dana could not always see the ghosts when they moved; they would be standing one place, then suddenly another.

"Aha!" Maude's voice echoed hollowly against the walls. "So something *is* going on between you two. Didn't I try to tell you, girls? You were a changed woman when you came back from that walk with Jake last night."

"Why wouldn't you tell us anything?" Rosella scolded.

"What happened on the walk?" Evelyn prodded.

Dana looked at the anxiety on their faces. How dear those faces were becoming to her. She couldn't lie.

"Jake thinks he is . . . Jake says he is in love with me."

"But this is wonderful!" Inez exclaimed, raising her hands into the air in a salute. And then, "That is, if you wanted to hear that, my dear. Did you?"

"Yes," Dana answered softly. "I love him, too."

"In such a short time?" asked Evelyn, her eyes like saucers.

"What is time?" said Rosella, the romantic. "I knew it the moment I saw them together. Knew this would happen. When it's right, it's right. This is no surprise to me."

From the pitch of her voice, Dana knew it was, indeed, a surprise. It was a surprise to all of them. Excitement crackled in the room like electricity.

"But this is wonderful!" Inez repeated.

Dana lowered her gaze. "Maybe not so wonderful. What can come of it when I live in a whole different world?"

"Then come to his world," suggested Rosella.

Dana's stomach dropped as if she had stepped onto a fast down elevator. Come to this crazy town? Leave the business she had struggled to build? Absurd!

For a man she loved?

For her new family that was unique in all the world?

Tears formed in Dana's throat. She had found nothing here in Devil's Fork but love! From these dear little ghosts. From Jake. Even from Nellie Jean. And yet, how could she ever belong here?

She got up, poured a glass of iced tea from the refrigerator and sat down next to the window. "I have two questions. First off, I want to know what will happen to all of you if we lose this house?"

The question had the effect of a storm warning. Frances replied, "We will get scattered. This house has been our bonding place for many years. There is no other place where we would all be connected and welcomed."

"Do you have to be welcomed?"

"Oh, yes, absolutely. We must be invited. We can't go where we are not invited, and I'm afraid no one else would take us all in. Even if we were able to ask, which we're not."

Dana was keenly aware of her own heartbeat, her own aliveness. These were not easy questions to ask, but she had to know just exactly what was at stake. "I didn't know spirits had to be invited."

Maude volunteered. "If spirits go where they aren't invited, they are unhappy. Obnoxious ghosts are the unhappy ones. The uninvited. We only want to live in peace here and keep up with the latest gossip. That's all we ask." Maude's eyes were so soft when she looked at her grand-niece it was easy for Dana to forget that they were not living eyes. "Now you are one of us, my dear, our connection to the earth plane. You are such a happy blessing for us."

Dana rubbed her tense neck muscles. "What you're saying is, you can't be together anywhere but here."

"That's right. In this house of mine—I mean yours. Now, there was another question? You said there were two."

Dana looked from one to the other. "I want to know if you have a secret that has to do with the town of Devil's Fork."

The ghosts' reaction to the question was swift and new. Rosella's legs stopped swinging. Frances stopped flipping at the flower on her hat. Evelyn turned her pink head of hair toward the window and avoided Dana's eyes. *There is a secret!* Dana thought, her heart jumping a beat.

"What are you talking about?" Louise asked.

"Nellie Jean told me the Ladies' Club was harboring a secret. Something you used to blackmail the town government for decades in order to achieve your own goals for the town."

"Why, how outrageous!" Rosella exclaimed.

"Scandalous!" agreed Evelyn.

Dana squared her shoulders. "Well, did your club or did it not control Town Hall?"

"Not directly, of course not," Maude answered.

"Indirectly?"

Maude paused. "Now and then we'd have a certain issue that concerned the citizens, and we made our stand clearly known. If that's what you mean."

"It isn't. I think you should let me in on whatever it is you know. I might be able to use it."

The ghosts looked at one another questioningly.

"We don't know anything about a secret," Louise said.

"Not a thing about a secret," agreed Frances.

Dana looked at her great-aunt challengingly. To her disappointment, Maude answered, "I don't know what convinced Nellie Jean we had a secret." As she said it, she looked away and would not meet Dana's eyes.

Dana caught the little ghosts exchanging concerned glances. *What the hell could be so secret they won't even talk about it from the spirit side?* she wondered. *What horrendous thing are they hiding?*

10

WHEN JAKE ARRIVED at seven, Dana felt as if she was seeing him for the first time again. She had forgotten how handsome he was and how captivating the smile she had seen so seldom. He was wearing jeans and a mint-green shirt. Her heart raced when the masculine scent of his after-shave reached her.

He did not kiss her in greeting. Instead, he handed her a bouquet of pink snowflakes and said, as if he had planned it, "They're the color of your dress."

"Thank you, Jake. I must find something to put them in."

He followed her through the hallway into the kitchen, where she set the wildflowers in a vase. Because the ghosts would be watching, Dana hurried him out of the house.

He led her to his pickup, held open the door and offered his hand to help her up the high step into the cab.

When he was settled in the driver's seat, Jake said, "You look beautiful."

Dana smiled and her eyes were drawn to his muscular thighs as he started the engine. How those thighs would photograph. "Where are we going?"

"To the Hidden Gulch steak house just west of town. Best prime rib in three counties."

"A popular place, is it? Aren't you worried that being seen there with me will stir up gossip?"

Jake laughed. "It'll stir up plenty of gossip."

"The gossip mongers watch you closely, I've learned."

"'Fraid so. I'm a public official."

"Handsome eligible bachelor," she corrected.

He glanced sideways at her. "Not eligible."

It stung a bit the way he said it. "Oh? *He said he was in love with me. What did "love" mean, if he doesn't consider himself eligible?*

Jake changed the subject. "Were you serious when you agreed to help with the ham-theft investigation?"

"Sure. Were you serious when you agreed to pose for me?"

"Yeah. It sounds like an okay exchange."

"Good. What do I have to do, and when?"

"Tomorrow you can do a stakeout near the meat counter at the First Street Market. Find excuses to hang around as long as you can. I'll make sure the butcher has a good selection of fresh hams, and it's your job to detect anyone watching the customers. Give me descriptions of suspects and I'll take it from there."

Dana leaned back in her seat and watched shadows of the trees pass by. "Wow. I never thought I'd get involved in a big-time crime investigation."

He laughed. "Big crime in Devil's Fork."

She closed her eyes. *I think this town is enchanted. It's like a magnet. The longer I stay—every hour I stay—I feel more a part of this crazy place.*

She shook the flashing thoughts away. "What motive could the thief have?"

Jake shrugged. "Maybe he just like hams, but I think it's more complicated than that, because no hams have disappeared from any of the stores. Only homes."

"I'll go to the market in the morning. After my police work, can we do a photo shoot?"

"I won't be any good at posing."

"You don't have to pose. Just carry on with your regular activities. The pictures are more natural that way."

They had driven through town and turned south. The Hidden Gulch, built of varnished log siding, lay in a clump of huge cottonwoods. Several cars were parked in front.

Inside the lights were dim, but a spotlight might as well have been on them—every eye stared. It was worse than Dana had imagined, but Jake was unrattled. She realized that by bringing her here, he was making a public statement. With his arm around her waist they entered the dining room. She could even hear the whispers.

During dinner he asked about Texas. "Do you photograph anything besides men in your studio?"

"At the moment, no. I've come to specialize in men. My preference is nature photography, but I couldn't make a living at it." Scenes flashed into her mind, unexpectedly: sunsets behind snowy mountains, a lazy river fed by mountain streams, bales of hay in yellow fields under an August moon, horses grazing in velvet green meadows. She could photograph all those things here—capture the beauty of Devil's Fork!

"Nature photography," he repeated thoughtfully. "Quite a difference from the calendar you showed me."

"I like many kinds of photography." *I could do proms and weddings and babies*, she thought. *I could do the winning animals at the county fair.*

"Dana," Jake said, sipping at his glass of wine, "you seem a little distracted. Are you worried about the house?"

"Yes. I'm afraid I won't be able to persuade your cousin to give me time enough."

"I'm afraid so, too. When I talked with him, he was so anxious to convince me there was no particular reason he wanted the property that I'm sure there *is* a reason. He has some scheme up his sleeve."

Dana looked up at his face, lit by the single candle flame on their table. "Can't you sway him, Jake? I have to have a little time!" *The secret*, she thought desperately. *If only I could find out the ghosts' secret!*

He gazed at her quizzically. "How much time do you need?"

Dana's mind was lifting off into space with wild thoughts. What if she made a phone call to Greenway Systems! Greenway had been begging to buy her property in Dallas for months because it bordered their main offices. She could command a high price in a minute. Probably three hundred thousand, against only a hundred and seventy in mortgage debt. More than enough for the taxes and for . . .

For *what*?

For restoring the house for the ghosts? For going into business as Devil's Fork's only photographer? For the chance to put colored film in her camera and photograph summer picnics and windmills against blue sky?

"Dana? I asked you how much time you'd need."

She heard a voice that sounded like hers reply, "Another two weeks. Maybe one if I really push it."

"Push what?"

Dana shook her head in confusion, feeling near tears with this mixture of frustration and excitement. *Push for the secret. Push for a sale of her business. I must be going mad!* The idea of changing her life hurt like a sharp arrow in her heart. But if there was no other way to save the house for the ghosts . . .

She gulped her wine. "I need time to decide what to do. But I'll do something. The house has . . . a hold on me."

He stared at her across the candlelit table.

"Jake, why are you looking at me like that?"

"I'm trying to figure you out. Why you'd want that house."

Her heart had begun to pound. She could hardly reply, *Because I have family there! Family who can't leave!* So she said weakly, "Because it's a fine old house."

He continued to stare. "But who would live in it?"

"I . . . I don't know." *I would!* the wild, arrow-shooting voice shouted inside her. Dana shivered at what the voice said. Then a calm descended over her like a warm cloak on a frosty morning, and she whispered, "Maybe I would."

Jake was silent for some seconds before he folded his hand over hers on the table. His hand was cold and then suddenly hot, his eyes held hers, and she was aware of his chest moving as he breathed.

"Dana, let's get out of here. Let's go home." His husky voice held a sensuous undercurrent.

"Home?"

"To my house. I want us to be alone."

"It's very dangerous, the thought of being alone."

He smiled. "I'm not dangerous. I told you last night how I feel about you. I'd protect you with my life. I'd never hurt you."

She felt his hand squeeze hers on the table.

He continued, "I want you, though. You can't know how much I want you."

"Maybe I can," she whispered, pushing back her chair.

Jake rose with her and took her hand as they left the dining room. She knew it was his way of telling the world, "This is the woman I have chosen."

The voice struck again, hard and fast. *Would you give this up?* it asked. *Would you give him up?*

Trees lined the narrow turnoff that led to his house. The lawn was green and shaded. Three dogs ran out to greet them, tails wagging furiously. Jake got out and gave them a sharp warning about jumping on guests.

Dana got only fleeting impressions of spacious rooms and sparse furniture as Jake led her through his house. Holding her hand, he took her down a hall to a wood-paneled room dominated by a king-size bed. Soft yellow light shone in from the hallway. So suddenly that she gasped, Jake pulled her into his arms and kissed her with such passion Dana lost all sense of balance and would have fallen had he not been holding her so tightly.

Once she had believed she knew what a man's touch could do to her—but she had *not* known, not until now. Until Jake. The wild mystery of him entered her body through every pore. His heart beat against hers and his hands moved in her hair and along the back of her neck.

"Jake . . ."

"Come to bed with me," he said in a ragged whisper.

His voice was pure seduction. She cupped his face with her hands and gazed unflinchingly into his eyes, trying to see into his soul. *No woman has ever really known this man,* she thought. But she could know him. His eyes were telling her that she alone could know him.

"Yes," she whispered. She felt his eyes drawing her to a place no one else had ever been, even as memory reminded her he had been married once to a woman long dead who had betrayed him.

He fumbled with her buttons, then lowered her dress over her shoulders. His hands moved over her skin, catching pink nylon straps between his fingers, and he bent to kiss her shoulders.

"You're trembling."

Her response was a shaky exhalation of her breath as his lips moved down her arm. "I've searched for you a long time, Dana. The first night we met, I think I fell in love in the midst of the blueberryderry crumbs."

She laughed softly. "How romantic! The truth is, I was falling in love, too, but I didn't want to admit it."

"Neither did I." He took her hands in his and began kissing her fingers gently, caressing each with his lips, completely absorbed in her.

Dana closed her eyes and shivered as Jake tasted her fingers, imagining how his skin tasted. Surely it would taste of the wild rambling river and the open field. . . .

She felt for the buttons of his shirt and undid them, trembling, desire building uncontrollably as the scent of his after-shave reached her and, as he bent, the clean smell of his hair brushing her face.

She let go of everything but him—every fear, every thought—let them float away, for Jake was here and he was real. When she pushed back the open shirt to reveal his bare chest, Jake helped her by untucking the tails and throwing the shirt carelessly onto the floor. He sat down on the bed, pulled off his boots, unbuckled his belt and wriggled out of jeans so tight they seemed a part of his body. Dana watched him peel off his brief undershorts and stand, holding out his arms to her. He pulled her close and held her. The warmth of his naked body heated her, even through the cotton dress.

Wherever he touched her, her body throbbed. She was tingling with runaway emotions, like bursts of fireworks that wouldn't stop. Her love for Jake MacGuire was the most overwhelming feeling she'd ever experienced.

Jake kissed her as he slid off her dress; her bra followed. His kisses lit a fire in her breasts. Dana closed her eyes while flames licked her body, over her ribs, her stomach—and lower as he knelt before her and slid off nylon lace before the path of his lips.

She wound her fingers in his thick hair as he held her with his arms around her hips and kissed her. When she swayed, he rose, sliding his body along hers like a wave of fire, then he lifted her as if she were weightless onto his bed.

"You feel so good against me," he said huskily. "Your body is like warm silk. I've imagined from the first moment I saw you how your body would feel against mine."

"When you first met me," she said, stroking his thick hair, "you seemed cold and aloof. I had been told you were standoffish, and you were. Do you try to be?"

"No, I don't try. I just don't go out of my way to be pleasant when I don't feel like it."

You must not feel like it very often, she said silently. People thought he was like his exterior—tough and cold. As he lay naked beside her, tender and aroused, she felt uniquely privileged to know a part of this man no others knew.

He caressed her gently, not hurrying, savoring each touch, kissing her spontaneously. His touch was so tender it brought tears to her eyes.

He asked, "Is something wrong?"

"No. It's just that you're arousing emotions that have long been buried. Your touch is so . . . loving."

His fingertips, following the contours of her body, moved along her inner thighs. "Why wouldn't my touch be loving? It comes with love."

Her heart soared. Maybe he meant it. Maybe the word "love" meant to him the same thing it meant to her! Was that possible? Could a man like this really have fallen in love with her? A man like this . . . A man bringing his lips toward hers again, in gentleness, giving her time. Giving them time.

She didn't need time to want him, only to know him, and he seemed to realize that, too. Folding his hand over hers, he guided her. "I want to feel your touch."

Her hands responded with new and bolder strokes. Exploring, tantalizing. Jake closed his eyes and moaned. "Touch of hot silk," he mumbled so softly she could barely hear.

He groaned again and struggled onto one elbow. "I didn't anticipate your magic, Dana. If you keep touching me like that, I'll explode. Here, love, come here to me." Urging her toward him, he kissed her—open-mouthed and hungrily. He lifted her over him.

Dana, trembling with new surges of passion, fit her body to his in an ultimate merging of body and spirit. She looked down into blue eyes blurred with the image of herself and saw love.

Only this man, her heart cried. *I want only this man and no other. There is no other and never will be.*

He whispered her name on the breath of a ragged sigh. It was more than an exhalation of passion; it was acceptance pure and total, of her, of them together.

Dana saw the shine of perspiration on his chest and his dark hair falling in his eyes; felt the warmth of his hands on her breasts and the strength of his body under hers. She felt his need so strongly that a sense of her own power overtook her. This was a man never before subdued, but in the heat of passion—for those fervent moments—he was giving over control to her! He was asking her to accept her power over him. Because he loved her.

Dana felt the power through all her being, remembering for the hundredth time his whispered words to her: *I don't know who you are, but I love you.*

Misty-eyed, her heart pounding, her breath catching erratically, Dana moved against him. She heard without hearing the call of a night dove outside, the soft rustle of wind in the trees, and she imagined the undulating movement of prairie grass in wind, and she moved with it, abandoning everything to the moment and the man who found the wind's rhythm with her.

She moved beyond fear and doubt or any thought into unimagined sensation, until Jake moaned and clasped her hands in his and held tightly, his eyes still closed. Ripples tore through her body and left her trembling. Her chest heaved. She watched Jake's eyelids flutter open. He gazed up at her and smiled softly as the tight grip of his fingers began to loosen.

Dana slid to his side and he held her close. "Ours is a merging of spirits," he whispered. "I can feel our spirits coming together—our hearts are not strangers and never were. I know that's true, though I don't know why. I only know I love you."

"I love you," she replied, her words muffled against his chest. She felt his heart beating.

They lay in silence while the shadows closed in and settled over them softly. Dana's inner voice once again nagged at her. *You would be a fool to leave him. And you are not a fool.*

Jake's breathing slowed as he relaxed. He ran his hands along her neck and shoulders and applied pressure with his fingertips. "Your muscles are tight across here. Tension?"

She moaned with pleasure. "That feels good."

"You're more worried than I realized."

"Of course I'm worried—about money and trying to stop your cousin from getting my house and tearing it down."

He shifted in the bed. "Here, let me massage these muscles for you. Just try to relax."

They lay in silence and she luxuriated in the rotation of his fingers until the pressure began to ease and the change in his breathing told her he had fallen asleep. Carefully she lifted his arm from across her shoulder, moved to the edge of the bed and rose. He was so soundly asleep he did not stir. She stood above him, watching him sleep and gazing at his handsome features, his husky well-proportioned body. The beauty of him was astounding.

Her heart reached out for his love. But a part of her drew back in fear. Would he love her as much if she did not live far away? If he believed she would stay in Devil's Fork?

. Or was he allowing himself to love her only because she didn't belong here? He had been betrayed in the past and had shown, through the years, no sign of wanting a commitment again. He had shown no sign of it now.

Would Jake feel threatened if she didn't leave? Would it scare him away? He was so beautiful in sleep. Dana smiled and gently lay back down, and he stirred and pulled her close.

Dana drifted on the edge of sleep with images of Devil's Fork floating in her mind; windmills and ice-skating in a frost-trimmed landscape, pink sunsets in the camera lens, Maude's old house painted in new summer white, her beloved family of ghosts waiting for her when she came home, Jake sleeping beside her. Zany, illogical town! It was winning her over with love.

11

A No Cats Allowed sign was posted on the door of the First Street Market. Dana entered behind a woman who walked in with a dog on a leash. Inside, at least three other people were shopping with dogs in tow.

She passed an elderly woman holding two sacks of potato chips for her mischievous-looking pug to sniff and asking, "Brutus, do you want the plain, or the sour cream and onion?"

A shrill bark came from the back of the store; a safe bet it was where the meat counter was located. Shoppers stood about, visiting. She caught snatches of conversations. The weather was hotter than last summer... Sunfish were biting in Toadfoot Lake... Jimmy Lee was seen in a new purple pickup....

The market was a busy place. Spotting a suspect might be more difficult than she had supposed. It could be a long morning; she wasn't meeting Jake until noon.

Because the meat counter was situated in the rear of the store, several aisles led to it, which helped; she could wander over a fairly large area and still see what was going on there. Dana didn't feel any of the intrigue associated with a criminal investigation in this atmosphere. A poodle sauntering down the aisle with its owner, gave Dana a "Aha! A stranger in the store look". A wag of its tail welcomed her.

"Now, Brutus, you behave," said the woman holding the poodle's leash. She smiled. "You're Dana French. I know you from your description. I'm Eleanor Binky— from over on Grape Street. I am sorry for your loss of your aunt Maude."

Dana looked down at the friendly little dog. "Brutus seems to be a very popular name for dogs."

"Oh my, yes. The most popular name—after our founding hero dog. We're very proud of our heritage."

And so it went during Dana's stakeout. People in the market were extraordinarily friendly, and welcoming, and all had something nice to say about Maude. It gave her a warm feeling. These smiles were genuine. How could one not like the people of Devil's Fork, even if they all had this odd thing about naming their dogs Brutus?

Nellie Jean came into the market with a toy dachshund on a leash. "Dana! What are you doing here?"

"Just getting acquainted with the town," she answered, looking at the dachshund. "I've always thought it was illegal to have dogs in food stores."

"A grossly unfair law. We make our own laws here."

"I've noticed." *Laws permitting taxes to go unpaid for decades, for example.* She leaned down to pet Nellie Jean's dog. "What's his name? Brutus?"

"No. I don't follow tradition. I'm a free thinker. My dog's named Rover." She paused. "What's so interesting at the meat counter? You keep looking over there."

Great spy I am, Dana thought with disgust. She said lamely, "There's a nice selection of meat."

"Speaking of which, I heard you and Jake had dinner at the Hidden Gulch last night. Wow! The whole town is talking. It makes you something of a heroine!

Prepare for some fierce glares from women who have their fantasies focused on the sheriff."

"I haven't noticed any fierce glares," Dana responded, praying Nellie Jean was not going to pursue this subject here, where the very shelves had ears.

"Good. Don't worry about it, anyway. Most people are really glad—for him, you know." Nellie Jean urged her dog away from the noodle packages on the bottom shelf. "I came for some macaroni. I've bought the elbow and the shell, and these wonderful alphabet-shapes. Also, I heard a truckload of watermelons has come in. I'm looking for someone to split one with me. Are you interested?"

"Not at the moment, no."

Dana was only half listening. She said, "That woman in the straw hat is buying two fresh hams. Who is she, anyway?"

"That's Wheatie Moran. She needs two, with a farmhand to cook for, as well as her five kids." Nellie Jean smiled a greeting at Wheatie. "Well, Rover has had his walk, and if I wait for a watermelon partner, I'll be late for work. Nice to see you." She tugged at the dog's leash and gave Dana a wave.

A few minutes later Dana spotted a middle-aged man in bib overalls and plaid shirt lurking near the meat counter, watching the customers, Wheatie Moran in particular, who had set the two hams in her grocery basket. She didn't like the way the man looked at Wheatie.

Her heart beat faster. Maybe he was the one! Trying to act nonchalant, Dana paced leisurely, adding an item or two to her own basket. The overall-clad man was watching the ham customers, no question about it! One or two people spoke to him, and he replied. Once he moved a short distance away and then came back. He did not buy any meat. By the time he left, Dana was certain the round-faced man was the ham thief.

Excitedly, she looked at her watch. There was no point standing around here any longer. Her mission was accomplished. It was only ten-thirty; she wasn't due to meet Jake at the park until twelve. That left plenty of time to drop the photos off at the mayor's office and have that little talk with Russell.

Nellie Jean wasn't in the reception office, but the inner door was ajar. Russell MacGuire was seated at his desk reading a newspaper. Dana knocked and let herself in.

His eyes went straight to the large manila envelope in her hand. "Dana! You have the photos. How'd they turn out?"

"I thought you'd like to see them for yourself."

"I've been waiting." He didn't rise, but motioned her to the chair in front of his desk.

She pulled them from the envelope and handed them to him. Russell studied the photos intently. Dana was sure he was thinking how handsome he was, and it was true. He looked clean-cut and successful. Although Dana thought he had the eyes of a schemer, he probably didn't see that.

"Yeah, they're good. Real good. Too bad they're not in color."

"I explained they wouldn't be."

"Yeah." He was bent over the photos, mesmerized. "I'd like to buy a copy of each."

"Okay. But our contract states that you can't do anything commercial with them."

"That depends on what you mean by commercial."

"You know perfectly well what it means. The contract spells it out."

"You are a connoisseur of men, Miss French. You really know what you like in a man, don't you?"

Discomfort surged in Dana. "Of course. It's my job. I want you to know I am considering using one of these photos for my calendar."

"Considering? I thought it was definite."

"No—there are others to choose from. I haven't made a final decision."

This took the wind out of his sails. He held up one. "I don't know how you could do any better than *this*."

She smiled. "I told you, I'm considering it. By the way, since I'm here, Russell, I thought I'd make that proposition to you again about the taxes. I'll pay off both Maude's debt and the taxes in installments."

"And keep the house? Why the devil would you want it?"

"I might ask you the same question."

"You did. I said I want the property, and unless that debt is paid, I can put it on public auction. That's just how it is."

"Not if you agree to my plan."

His cheeks reddened and he looked frustrated. He glanced at the top photo and then back at her. "I can't. The town is demanding on the money for the pool."

"No, *you* are," she countered coolly. "Your construction company is what's holding up the works. You could take installments if you wanted to."

"And if I don't?"

"If you don't, then I'll have to find the cash."

To say he looked crestfallen was not an exaggeration. *Why does he want my house so badly?* she wondered. Abruptly she picked up the photos and slid them into the envelope.

He rose, red-faced. "I thought you didn't have the cash."

"There are ways."

He swallowed. Anger showed in his eyes, but his voice remained controlled. "This won't influence the calendar decision, surely. I mean, this is great stuff here! You did a fabulous job with these."

"I did, didn't I? They make you look like a movie star, Russ. But I don't know. Right now I'm too busy worrying about the house to make that decision."

This was not going the way he wanted, but Dana saw he wouldn't bend. Jake was right; there was a reason— a big reason—why Russell wanted Maude's property.

He said, "Order me a copy of those pictures, okay? I want one to put up in the courthouse."

"Sure—as soon as I get a chance."

Russell came around the desk. "Will you have dinner with me tonight?"

"Sorry. I already have a date."

"With my cousin? Hell, break it. I'm the man you want—a mayor, not a sheriff." He touched her arm and moved so close she thought he was going to try to kiss her.

She shot out of the chair, grabbed the pictures and stepped back. "I'm doing a photo shoot with Jake." Russell deserved the jab.

His mouth curled with anger. "Not for September, I hope!" It sounded like a threat.

But he had set himself up. "Maybe," she answered wickedly. "I won't know for sure until I see the photos."

She turned her back on him and rushed out of the office barely able to contain her fury. He had had the gall to make a pass at her! And to act like he owned September.

His mistake.

BIRDS WERE SINGING in the tall trees that shaded the park. The soft summer air was filled with the fragrance of flowering bushes. The sky was cloudless, even over the distant mountain peaks. Dana was glad it was still too early to meet Jake at their designated meeting place by the picnic table, because she needed time to cool down, and time to think.

She strolled through the quiet green park seething over Russell's refusal to help, and the way he had talked about his cousin. Russell, she had discovered, was a louse. She would like to help Nellie Jean find a way to take over as mayor; she was virtually running the mayor's office, after all.

What horrendous secret was being kept by the ghosts that enabled them to control this whole town?

Whatever it was, Dana intended to have another go at finding out. But she couldn't count on that secret to get her out of this mess. There was only one way.

The flower-lined path led to a shaded play area with a slide and swings. The park was deserted on this summer day, except for a boy and his dog playing ball on the green. Dana settled into one of the swings.

The situation was simple: either she came up with the cash or the ghosts would lose their home and be scattered Lord knew where, and she would never see any of them again. They loved her and they needed her; no one else could help them.

Dana pushed at the grass with her feet and the swing moved. In a moment, she was pumping slowly. There was only one thing she could do. Sell the building in Dallas and see if she could make a go of her business here.

It might work. She could still do the calendars, although it might take a bit more searching to find models. And she could do the nature photography she had always dreamed of. And as for local weddings and proms, why not? Didn't Devil's Fork deserve the best? Certainly it would cost her less to live; the house would be paid for once the tax bill was out of the way. Profit from the building in Dallas would leave her plenty to set up her business, make necessary repairs on the house and carry her until her reputation as a photographer was established.

Devil's Fork. Was she mad to think of living here?

For two days the idea had been building momentum. Her only family was here—the lovable ghosts. And Jake was here. And the people—all but the scheming mayor—made her feel welcome. As she swung, she felt the tension fall away and joy take its place. As soon as lunch with Jake was over, she would call Dallas. If she told Greenway Systems she had to have forty thousand this week, they would be calling a broker in minutes; they'd been pleading for a chance to buy that building for months. Okay, decided! The ghosts would have their home, and her with it. Joyfully, she pumped herself higher in the swing.

And Jake? What would he say? Everyone claimed he was obsessed with discovering who his wife's lover was, the man who was there when she was killed. He still thought about the betrayal, was still determined to find out the truth, and until he did, he wouldn't get too involved. All the gossip said this. Inez had hinted at it. It was safe for him to love her because he thought she was temporary. If she were a permanent resident of this town, she would be to him like all the other women— a threat to his freedom.

This thinking is illogical, Dana told herself as the swing slowed down. Illogical, maybe, but it was strongly intuitive. She was going to stay in Devil's Fork, but she had to be prepared for the possibility that Jake might turn away from her when he found out.

No need to tell him yet. Better to wait until after she had talked to the people in Dallas to make sure the plan was going to work.

The boy who was playing in the park had wandered over to the playground, his spotted dog running along behind. "Hi," he said shyly.

"Hi." She smiled.

He bounced the ball and it went rolling through the grass. "Want a push?"

"Sure!"

Not since childhood had she felt the sensation of swinging high in a swing, with the warm breeze in her face and her hair flying. *The place is enchanted.* She laughed inside herself. A mixture of peace and excitement came with the realization that she was really going to stay.

"High enough?" the boy asked.

"High enough," she answered. And added, "Your dog is cute. What's his name?"

"It's a she," the boy answered with a grin. "Her name is Brutus."

Jake came down the path at a fast clip, then picked up the ball, barely pausing, and threw it for the dog, then greeted the boy by name. The boy threw the ball back and forth with Jake a few times, and then went off to play in the field where two more boys had shown up.

Jake took Dana's hand as she got off the swing. "There's a hot-dog wagon across the park. Do you want a hot dog?"

"Sure." She squinted at him. "You haven't asked about the stakeout."

"I figured you'd tell me if you turned up a suspect."

"I turned up *the* suspect. A man in his late forties, short, round face, red cheeks, and he was wearing bib overalls and a blue-and-red plaid shirt with holes in both elbows."

"That's Harve Hankerman! But I can't see Harve as the serial thief."

"I'll bet he is. He was really eyeing the people buying hams, and he spoke to one or two of them. He'd go off and then come back and watch some more, and he didn't buy any meat. Is he a farmer?"

"He was until he got a bad back and had to sell his farm. He lives over on Cougar Street with his pet pig. He's been fighting Town Hall over that pig. There's an ordinance against having pigs in the town limits, and Harve refuses to get rid of his. Says it's part of his family."

"Then why can't the town be kind and bend the rule?"

"For a pig? People here have no tolerance for pigs. Especially the mayor."

Dana shook her head, confused. "You'd think a man who likes pigs wouldn't be such a glutton for ham."

"Yeah, you'd think so. Is he your only suspect?"

"Yes."

Jake smacked his lips thoughtfully. "Okay. We'll put a tail on him and see what happens."

They walked in silence down the path through the quiet little park. "Thanks, Dana."

"You're welcome. I think I like working on criminal cases."

He laughed. After a time he said, "I can't stop thinking about you—about last night."

Butterflies formed in Dana's stomach and began their little dance at the memory of him. Of their night together.

"Last night was wonderful," he continued in his husky voice that told her he was aroused thinking about it, too. He squeezed her hand and looked at her. "I get off work at five."

"Won't you be tailing your major suspect?"

"I'll let my deputy have that job."

She imagined his king-size bed and Jake lying back against the pillows, naked and wanting her. Reaching out to her . . . The butterflies were out of control. Dana looked into his seductive blue eyes. "I'll wait for you, then,' she promised.

DANA SAT IN THE CENTER of a circle of ghosts. They were all gazing at her in stunned silence. Maude was the first to speak.

"But Dana, my dear! Are you sure?"

"Absolutely sure. Now that I know all of you, how can I leave you? I don't want to leave you."

The hush remained. The ghosts were looking at each other and at her.

"And I want this house," Dana added. "It's beautiful!"

"It's wonderful that you would consider it," her aunt said.

"It's beyond consideration. It's decided. I telephoned Dallas from town. A realtor is drawing up the contracts, and I can sign by fax. I expect a check in the mail in a few days."

Maude was subdued. "You sold your building to pay my back taxes?"

"They're my taxes now. You gave them to me. And yes, it's the only way."

"But can you be happy in Devil's Fork?"

"I already am happy in Devil's Fork." As she looked at the faces around her, the happiness her news had generated rose like sprinkles of stardust in the room.

"I feel like dancing!" Rosella exclaimed, raising her chubby arms and whirling weightlessly through the room.

"Me, too!" declared Evelyn, kicking up her heels.

In a moment they all were swirling around her as gracefully as wisps of smoke. It seemed as if music came in from some mysterious other place and filled the house. Beautiful, ghostlike music that caught Dana in its spell. She laughed and twirled with them, dancing and dipping, and tried to hold the ladies' hands, but it was like gripping air.

"We're together!" Louise cried, leaping, in her enthusiasm, right over Dana's head.

"Together," Dana echoed, dancing her way across the room like a ballerina, until her toe caught in the wheel of Maude's Queen Anne tea cart, tipped it and sent the tea set flying. Rosella was close enough to help the china land on the rug without breaking, although Dana had no idea how she did it.

The ladies dissolved in laughter, and Dana laughed with them. She was fully aware that it was too easy to forget what a unique club she'd joined. It was the most wonderful thing that had ever happened to her, and she couldn't tell anyone about it, not even Jake.

When the laughter subsided, Maude said, "If I were alive, I would fix lemonade and cookies for a celebration."

"I can fix lemonade and open the box of sugar cookies I bought," Dana said. "And I'll enjoy them for all of us."

The ghosts sang their approval. In the kitchen, Dana waited for what she thought was the right moment—when everyone was happily celebrating—to bring up *the subject* again.

She began cautiously. "So. Now that we're all together for good, isn't there something you gals want to share with me?"

"Our laughter and our love," Frances said in her poem-reading voice.

"No. Something else. I'm talking about your big secret."

A hush fell. The ladies definitely didn't like this subject

Inez said, "Just because Nellie Jean thinks there's some big secret doesn't mean there is one."

"Nellie Jean knows everything about this town."

"Except *that*," Rosella said, then quickly slapped her hand over her mouth as the others glared at her.

"There, you see?" Dana said. "There is a secret, and since I am one of you, I think I should know it."

"Why?" asked Evelyn, still glaring at Rosella.

Dana hesitated. She wanted to point out that Nellie Jean needed the secret to dethrone Russell MacGuire, but here was Inez, Russell's grandmother, standing before her with such happiness and love in her pale eyes. It wouldn't do to go into all the reasons Russell was too underhanded and untrustworthy to hold the town's highest office. Dana couldn't push the issue without hurting Inez.

Louise said weakly, averting her eyes, "If we did have a secret, we would have to have a meeting and vote on telling it."

"That's so," agreed Frances. "If we did know a secret it would be an extremely serious secret, or we wouldn't keep it so well hidden."

"I understand," Dana said, disappointed, but grasping this thin straw of hope. "You couldn't divulge any serious secret—if you had one—without voting. It's a club thing. Okay. Will you have a meeting?"

"Not that we *do* have a secret," Rosella said, finally removing her hand from her mouth.

"I know. I know. But think about it, will you?" Any mention of their secret seemed to frighten the ghosts. It was a lulu, whatever it was. Dana knew they were not going to let go of it very willingly, if at all. It would have to be a unanimous vote.

Discouraged over their denial, she rose from her chair and looked at the clock. "I have to wash my hair and get ready. Jake is picking me up in less than two hours."

This announcement caused the chatter to begin—like the sound of bees buzzing louder and louder.

"Aha!" Rosella said. "Another date! Good. Excellent. Where's he taking you?"

"I don't know. He didn't say."

"Romance! Ah, sweet romance! It's in the air, ladies."

"Jake is a very nice young man," Maude confirmed.

"Very nice," his grandmother agreed.

But as she said it, Dana noticed a sadness in her eyes. "What is it, Inez?"

The little ghost hesitated in answering. "Oh, it's just that other thing. That thing with Jake's wife, Caroline. He's acted so differently ever since that happened. One of the last things he told me just before I crossed over was that he would never marry again. Of course, that was just after it happened, but from what I've heard about him since he seems to have meant it."

"I was afraid of that," Dana said. "I've sensed it." She did not want to talk about the prospect of marrying Jake. It had not come up and probably wouldn't, and the thought of losing him was more than she could bear. Especially now, anticipating being with him tonight, so soon . . . again.

"Well," she said with a great sigh and a forced smile, "I have to get ready." She removed the antique eyeglasses before Jake's name could come up again and ran up the stairs.

At five-twenty, he arrived at her door, still dressed in his uniform. The badge sparkled in the sun as he stood there smiling. Without a word, he reached out and took her in his arms and kissed her.

Dana drowned in his kiss, opening her mouth over his, feeling his tongue hard against hers. Her heart went wild.

Oh Lord, the ghosts are watching! she thought suddenly, horrified, and tried to pull away. His grip was tight. His kiss intensified, his hands moving up and down her back. *No!* she screamed in silence, but she could not stop her body from responding to the heat of his.

"I could think of nothing but you all day," he said.

"Tell me," she murmured.

"Tell *me*. Say you want me as much as I want you."

"Does my body lie?" she whispered hoarsely.

"No," Jake smiled, and bent to kiss her again.

She struggled weakly.

"Why are we standing here on the porch, Dana? Aren't you going to ask me in?"

"Uh, well, I thought we were going to dinner."

"We are. Later. The night's just beginning, and I've missed you all day. Right now, I'd just like to hold you in my arms and kiss you all over and make love to you."

Her cheeks flushed bright red. *Here? In this house with the ladies of the club spying on them?* Her knees went weak.

Jake said, "You're trembling, Dana. Hell, so am I."

"I . . . we can't . . ." she stammered.

"Can't? You haven't changed your mind about us?"

"No." She shook her head self-consciously. "It's just that we can't—" She stopped. How could she explain the unexplainable? Jake was going to begin to think she was crazy.

"Jake, can we go to your house?" she said so softly he could barely hear.

"Is there something wrong with yours?"

"No...yes... I'm just not comfortable in this house. I think it might be haunted."

Jake laughed. "If it is, that makes it all the more fun, doesn't it?"

"I don't want any ghost bothering us."

He laughed again and leaned close, straining to hear. "Why are you whispering?"

She shrugged self-consciously and continued in a whisper, "I would be more comfortable at your house. Like before."

"I don't know how you can stay here alone, Dana, if you think the house is haunted and you're afraid of the ghost."

She flushed and tried to push him away from the doorway. "I didn't say I'm afraid. But there are some things that are just none of their...its business."

Jake looked at her strangely. "Okay, sweet. My house it is. But this sounds like something we should discuss. Next time."

Next time? She couldn't keep Jake away from her house indefinitely. The problem seemed insurmountable. Now, with passion shining in his eyes and the fire in his fingers when he touched her, she didn't want to think about it; she just wanted the safety and warmth of Jake's arms.

In the driveway, the radio in his police pickup began squawking and cracking loudly. Jake's head jerked around.

"What is it?" Dana asked.

"It has to be my deputy," he answered, taking her hand and leading her down the steps. "Something must be happening with our theft suspect."

Dana pulled back long enough to close the front door. She had learned there was no point in locking it— not in Devil's Fork. "What's the big hurry?"

"There must be a theft in progress," Jake answered, walking in such long strides Dana could barely keep up. "This probably means we've got the guy, Dana. Come on. Let's go!"

Once they were on the road he turned on the siren. He drove so fast, she had to hang on to whatever she could find to keep from falling across the seat when he turned a corner. Jake was talking on the radio the whole time.

Their destination was a house just inside the city limits. "Right in Harve's neighborhood," Jake said, pulling into the driveway. Deputy Fargo came running out of the bushes to meet them.

"He's in the house, Sheriff! The Clancys aren't home!"

Jake threw open the truck door and ran inside. Dana sat spellbound. A real police arrest, and *she* had been the one to finger the suspect!

Seconds later the sheriff and his prisoner emerged from the house, walking side by side. No gun, no hands raised, no reading of rights. They just walked out, and the thief—the man she had spotted—was talking animatedly. Jake was listening patiently. In a few moments, the thief and the ham went off with Deputy Fargo, and Jake got back in the truck and started the engine.

"Now," he said. "where were we?"

She pushed at his elbow. "Jake! You've just apprehended Devil's Fork's major criminal! What were you and the thief talking about? Did he say why he did it?"

"Yeah. He's mad at the town because the mayor has insisted on enforcing the ordinance against allowing pigs. Harve says he's fighting the ordinance. Says he and his pig intend to make sure no one is comfortable buying hams. It's his protest—his and the pig's."

Dana tried to control her giggles. She ought to be getting used to one ridiculous surprise after another in this town. "Jake, how do you feel about that pig ordinance?"

"I think the city should have made an exception in Harve's case. He's got a damn smart pig there. But people here hate pigs and don't want one living in their town. That law has been on the books for a long time. Besides, Harve had the nerve to name his pig Brutus, which incensed everybody, especially Russell who identifies personally with the legend." He laughed. "To Russ, naming a pig Brutus is a criminal act."

He laid his hand on Dana's knee as he turned out of the drive. "Thanks for the detective work. You're the one who cracked the case."

She laughed. "I guess I should have become a private eye."

She held her breath as they approached her driveway, but he didn't turn in. Thank heaven. They were headed for his house, as she had suggested. Hopefully he wouldn't remember her reasons for not wanting to make love in her house, but of course he would remember. The matter would come up again and again, because now she had decided to live there. She knew she was in for some awkward times ahead.

Jake said, "We'll have dinner at my place and then relax and watch the moon come up. Don't worry, m'love. No ghosts will be prowling at my house. There will only be you and me and the moonlight."

12

THE NEXT MORNING Jake left his office at ten o'clock and walked the block and a half to the bank. He knew his sudden need for thirty thousand dollars would arouse suspicion. But he couldn't see any other way to help Dana keep that house. She'd said she was able to make payments, so she could make them to the bank. He would absorb the interest himself. If she owned a house in Devil's Fork, it would be a first step in cutting her ties with Texas. Jake was determined to keep her in his life no matter what it took.

It wasn't going to be easy asking the bank for a loan, especially when he couldn't explain what he needed the money for. The bank president, Sloan Wills, would just have to let him sign over a few acres of his land as collateral and not ask questions. Sloan wouldn't have the nerve to turn him down, but tongues were sure going to wag if anyone got wind of this. The hell with wagging tongues. She was worth it. Jake knew Russell too well; Dana was running out of time.

DANA AROSE LATE and came down for coffee with her hair tangled and circles under her eyes. When she felt the presence of her boarders in the kitchen, she slid on the glasses. They were all there, and buzzing.

"You came home awfully late, dear," said Rosella with a wink. "You were at Jake's house, were you?"

"Now, Rosella, we mustn't be too inquisitive," Frances said, wagging her head. "After all, Dana doesn't have to answer to us for anything."

"True, true," agreed Evelyn authoritatively. "Dana has saved our house for us, and we'll not forget we are her guests!"

"You aren't my guests," Dana countered, measuring coffee for the pot. "You ladies lived here first. I consider us all equal partners in this arrangement."

"And confidantes," Rosella added eagerly. "Tell us about last night!"

"Jake caught the serial ham thief."

Inez smiled proudly. "Was it Harve, like you said?"

"Yes. Caught red-handed. He said he did it to protest that city ordinance against resident pigs."

"Oh, tell us every detail!" Louise pleaded.

Rosella had other things on her mind. "Not now. We want to hear about you and Jake. Are you going to marry him?"

"You're being premature," Frances scolded.

"Very," Dana said.

"Well, you are in love with him!"

Dana brushed her hair from her face, thinking of last night. Of lying in Jake's arms with the light of the full moon shining through the window of his bedroom. "I wish it were that simple."

"He must be very pleased to know you're staying in Devil's Fork," Maude said.

"I haven't told him."

"Why not?"

"I'm afraid it'll scare him away. I think I'm afraid of his past. He still doesn't know who his wife was running away with, and that haunts him. Whenever the subject comes up, I see this awful anger in his eyes."

"Betrayal is a terrible thing," Inez said, shaking her head.

"The issue just isn't closed for him." Dana sighed.

"It's because he never caught the guy!" Rosella blurted. "That's the thing. He never knew who was with Caroline. He has never been able to take his anger out on anybody."

"He doesn't think he's ready for marriage again," Dana said.

"Did he say so?"

"He mentioned once that he isn't eligible, which is the same thing. He isn't afraid to love. He even admits he needs love, but if he thought I were anything but temporary, he'd back off."

"You don't know that," Evelyn insisted.

"No, I don't know that. Tonight I'll tell him. It's just taken me a day to work up the courage."

Louise began pacing the kitchen floor. "What we need, girls, is the name of Caroline's lover. That would clear the slate so Jake could get on with his life."

"Oh, sure. But how?" Evelyn looked disgusted.

They all discussed Dana's problem except Inez who became strangely quiet. Soon the others were looking at her. At last Rosella raised a plump, accusing finger. "Inez MacGuire, you know something!"

The old woman's eyes were sad. "You all know very well it does no good for a spirit to know something. A ghost's information is of no use to anyone, because no one would believe where it came from."

They crowded around her. Dana felt her heartbeat quicken. "You *do* know something!"

"Yes. But it would only frustrate you to know, my dear, because the information is useless to you."

"Maybe it wouldn't be! I could help Jake find out, maybe. Oh, please, Inez, if you know who he is, please tell us."

Louise was shaken. "Do you mean to say that all this time you knew who Caroline's lover was and didn't tell us? How could you not tell us?"

"Because there's nothing to be gained. Dana can't use the information."

"Let me decide what to do with it," Dana said. "Please."

Jake's grandmother sighed and seemed to settle deeper into the chair. "Very well, then. For Dana's sake. For what she has done for us. But I feel shame about it, which is why I've been silent. In the last days before I crossed over, Caroline MacGuire sat beside my sickbed and talked to me. We were close in many ways, and she was upset. She told me Jake was working long hours in the construction company with Russell, and she had become involved with someone else. For a long time she wouldn't tell me who he was. But in those last days, she said the two of them had plans to go to Denver for a week to be alone and figure out what they were going to do. It was then she told me the man she had fallen in love with was Russell."

Groans of despair circled the room. "Surely not Russell!" Maude exclaimed. But Dana was not surprised. Russell would have been her first guess, especially after the way he tried to move in on her after he knew she had dated Jake.

"You can understand why I didn't want to tell," Inez continued. "Russell is my grandson, and I love him. But

I also know about his mischief. I have seen it often. At the time I learned this, I was too ill to tell Jake. Caroline knew that. The next day the car flipped over on the ice and she was found dead. Soon after, I myself made the transition."

Dana knew she couldn't openly accuse Russell of such a thing. Jake was close to his cousin and trusted him, at least in most of the ways men trust each other. Something had to be done, though. She couldn't sit on information like this. On the other hand, what was she to do? Say a ghost told her?

"I have to figure out what to do with this," she said to the ladies.

"Think, girls!" demanded Maude.

A silence prevailed. No one had an answer.

Dana sipped her coffee. Finally she said, "There's no choice. I'm just going to tell him, that's all. I'll prepare him the best way I can and then spring it on him about you gals. *Can* I tell him about you all?"

They looked at one another. "We don't keep ourselves a secret," Frances said. "Jake is a skeptic about such things as spirits, though."

"So let him use the glasses," Rosella said, as if the matter were as simple as that. "We all agree we want Dana to marry this man, and she won't be able to keep us a secret from him. As far as I'm concerned, he might as well know now."

"Is this agreeable to everyone?" Maude asked.

The ghosts raised their arms in the air. A club vote. Unanimous approval.

Dana said, "Okay. Jake and I will have a serious talk and I'll explain about all of you, and then I'll allow him to see you. And then I'll tell him about Caroline and

Russell. Oh Lord, I don't know what he'll do! He's so famous for his temper."

"He is that," Inez agreed.

Dana took a deep breath for courage. "Jake said he would be here after work to pick me up. I offered to cook dinner at his house, but I'll tell him I've changed my mind and we are going to have dinner here. Then I'll sit him down and tell him."

JAKE WALKED OUT of the Prairie Chicken Saloon stirred up by a compelling need for Dana. Loving her was like being given a new life, like awakening from a long dark night to the light. Blinding light. As he'd listened to Preacher Donald's love songs, he'd thought of nothing else but her.

He was feeling the emotional songs and the beers, and relishing the thought of telling Dana he had arranged for a loan so she could keep her house. Tonight, after they made love, he would pour a drink and spring it on her. Afterward they would make love again. It was going to be a memorable evening!

The moment she opened the door, he swept her into his arms and rained kisses on her face. "What a woman you are!"

Dana, who had been waiting in dread of the bombshells she had to drop on him tonight, was caught off-guard. *Wait. Don't get amorous right now,* she thought desperately. She had to concentrate on the tasks at hand.

"You have beer on your breath," she said, trying to puncture his mood.

"I've been at the Prairie Chicken celebrating life and passion with the preacher."

"A preacher at the saloon?"

"He sings great songs. Maybe we'll go later and hear him. Much, much later." He kissed her on the mouth.

As always, his kiss caught her in its promise and its spell. Dana reeled and then gently tried to push him away. This was not the time!

"Dana, what's wrong?"

"I need to talk to you, Jake . . ."

"Okay, we'll talk," he agreed distractedly. He reached out to touch her hair and slide his fingers along her neck. "After I kiss you again."

His lips were warm and loving, but Dana couldn't fully appreciate the taste of him when her body was like a tightly drawn wire.

"Jake—"

"I want you," he muttered.

He swept her up in his arms and carried her through the foyer and up the stairway.

"What are you doing?"

"I'm doing Rhett Butler. If he could take matters into his hands, so can I."

"Wait!" she demanded, but like Rhett, he paid no attention.

In the wide upstairs hallway, all the doors but one were closed. He carried her into that room, Maude's bedroom—now Dana's—and laid her on the bed.

"Jake, we can't do this. You don't understand—"

"I'm not concerned about ghosts. All I need to understand is that we love each other and I want you."

She squirmed as he snuggled down next to her and began to caress her. She fought off the desire to lose herself in his love. "No, Jake, not now and not *here!*"

"On your bed? What's wrong with that?"

She tried to push him away, but he was too heavy. "No, not like this. We have to talk seriously."

"We can talk later."

"Darn it, I—"

A ringing interrupted her. Dana said, "That's the phone. It's downstairs in the kitchen."

"There's no phone upstairs?"

"No." Dana struggled to get off the bed. "It could be Dallas. I've been waiting for a call. Business. Which I'll explain. I have to get it." She got to her feet, brushing her hair from her eyes. "Come down, Jake, and I'll make us a drink."

He was not behind her as she ran down the long stairs, nor anywhere in sight when she reached the kitchen. Maybe it was just as well. Dana was certain the call was confirmation that her building sale was closed, and since she had already faxed her signature the buyer was as anxious as she was, and had the cash.

"Hello?"

"Dana, Russell MacGuire here. I have some business to talk over with you."

The voice was cold. For a second she was afraid he knew she'd found out he'd been Carolyn MacGuire's lover, but the rush of fear quickly evaporated. He couldn't possibly know.

He continued, "I have an offer to make on your house that you won't want to refuse."

The panic Dana felt wasn't explainable. Maybe it was the sound of his voice. "I told you, the house isn't for sale."

"I insist you listen to my offer just the same. I'm coming out tonight so we can discuss it."

The panic rose. "No. Not tonight. I'll come to your office first thing in the morning. We can talk then." By that time, she was certain, the check would be on its way and they could be done with all this.

Russell replied, "Won't do. I have a meeting in the morning, and this can't wait. It won't take long. I'll be out in an hour, maybe less."

"Russell, don't—" she began, and heard the click of the receiver. She felt a chill of fear. What did he really want? There wasn't a minute to waste. Jake had to be told she was staying. He had to be told everything, and fast.

Dana's mouth was dry. She poured herself a glass of water and drank it down, aware that what she dreaded most was Jake's reaction. What would he do to Russell?

Jake had not come down as she had asked him to. When she called to him from the bottom of the stairs, he didn't answer. Maybe her voice wouldn't carry that far, but more likely he just wanted her back in the bedroom. He was really in a mood!

Jake was in a mood, all right. All day he had been thinking of tonight, of her in his arms, and the sight of her at the door in her tight jeans and flowered sleeveless blouse had done him in. With the songs of love still in his head, he wanted to make love to her once again and feel her passionate response. He had denied himself love for so long that now it was like a dam unleashed. He couldn't get enough of her.

Cursing the phone, he kicked off his boots, unzipped his jeans and undressed. He pulled back the bedspread and fluffed the pillows, then arranged himself comfortably—as comfortably as was possible with his blood burning hot in anticipation of her and his body aching. There would be no more stalling when she came back in and saw that he was ready and waiting.

He heard her call from downstairs. That meant she was off the phone. He didn't answer. For a short time the house was eerily silent. Then she called his name again, from the top of the stairs this time, and he heard her soft footsteps in the hall.

· At the bedroom door, Dana halted and gasped when she saw him lying naked on her bed.

"Jake!"

He grinned. "Hey, why are you looking at me like that, Dana? What am I, the big bad wolf?" He reached for his undershorts and arranged them on his head like a nightcap. In what he considered his most wolflike voice, he growled, "The better to snuggle with. Come to bed, my pretty one . . ."

Dana stood paralyzed, a look of horror on her face. "Jake! Omigod . . . omigod . . ."

Jake was not listening to her. He bared his teeth in a frightening grin. "The better to bite you with, my dear." Growling, he grabbed the pair of antique eyeglasses from the bedside table and set them on his nose. "The better to *see* you with my—"

Jake froze. Standing around the bed were a bunch of little old ladies! One . . . two . . . three . . . *six* of them! All of whom he knew, and all of whom he knew were dead. Including Granny MacGuire and weird old Maude O'Connor, his third-grade teacher. Ghosts. The lot of them.

The noise he emitted was scarcely human. He bolted upright, yanked his shorts off his head and pulled them on while Dana screeched, "Take the glasses off and you won't be able to see them!"

"Ghosts?" he gasped while he frantically struggled into his jeans. *"Ghosts?"*

"Yes," she answered, overcome with embarrassment for him.

"They look so damned . . . real!" He shook his head as if to throw off the vision and pulled off the glasses. His eyes were wild. Dana took the spectacles from him and dropped them into the pocket of her blouse.

"They're real, Jake. They live here. That's why I couldn't get rid of the house—because of them."

He was staring at her as if she were speaking a language he couldn't understand. "What the hell are you talking about?" His voice was without its usual strength.

"Didn't you recognize them?"

He didn't answer. The last thing in the world he wanted to do was recognize them. And yet he had.

"The ladies of the Ladies' Club," Dana was saying. Her voice was trembling and she rambled nervously. "My great-aunt and your grandmother among them. It's possible to see them but only with those glasses on. I don't know why. I can't explain it. I only know that when I came here, I put on the glasses because Aunt Maude left them in a place where I would find them right away, and I discovered that the ladies are here."

Jake was stunned and silent. *The Ladies' Club? Now ghosts?* Lurking around this house and watching Dana? Watching *them?* No wonder she'd been so determined they not make love in this house! No wonder she'd tried to stop his amorous advances! His hands shook as he struggled with his boots. He asked, "Is this some kind of trick, Dana? Are you able to create illusions, along with your other psychic gifts?"

"You mean the blueberryderries and the lullaby and the towel and all that? Hardly psychic gifts, Jake. Your grandmother told me about those things. I've come to know all the ghosts, and they're wonderful and sweet and a lot of fun. Damn it, if you'd listened to me and come downstairs, you wouldn't have been so embarrassed."

"Embarrassed is not a strong enough word," he muttered angrily. "Why the hell didn't . . ." His voice trailed off.

"I was going to tell you. Remember I kept saying I wanted to tell you something? I was trying hard to keep you out of the bedroom, if you recall."

He rushed into the hall and headed for the stairs.

She said, "The ghosts aren't confined to the bedroom."

"I need a drink."

She followed as he bounded down the stairs three steps at a time. "What you need, Jake, is to sit still and listen to me. It isn't just the ghosts. There's more I want to tell you."

"I don't think I can take any more."

In the kitchen Dana opened a beer, and handed it to Jake, who sat pale and quiet at the table.

Guzzling the beer, he asked, "Have I lost my mind?"

"Of course not, you've just seen a few ghosts. Don't ask about the glasses. I haven't a clue why they—"

"They were talking, Dana! Ghosts talking and giggling like a bunch of teenagers!"

"Why wouldn't they be? You gave them plenty to giggle about."

"Damn it! And I thought you were imagining a ghost in this house."

She sat down across the table from him and took his hand. It felt unnaturally cold. "Look, there isn't time to discuss the details of this unusual phenomenon. Not right now. I really must talk to you. For the few seconds you wore the glasses, did you recognize your grandmother among the ghosts?"

He held his head as if he were in pain. "Yes, but I thought I was losing my mind."

"You aren't. She's lovely, Jake. And she loves you."

His expression was blank. "I can't deal with this, Dana."

"You have to deal with it, and you have to deal with it quickly, because there's more. Your grandmother could tell you herself if you put on the glasses and talked to her . . . Jake, are you listening?" she asked the top of his head.

He nodded weakly.

Glancing worriedly at the clock, Dana swallowed. "Your grandmother knows who your wife's lover was. She told me."

His head jerked up. "What did you say?"

Dana struggled to keep calm. "Try to hold your temper, Jake, please. Inez told me Caroline talked about the other man and their plans to go to Denver for a week to decide what to do."

Jake's stare burned into her skin. This was one of the most difficult things she had ever done, and maybe the timing was bad, but it was too late to stop now. Minutes were passing and Russell was on his way.

Jake grabbed her hand. His voice was flat and cold. "What are you trying to tell me, Dana?"

"Your grandmother told me her lover was your cousin."

The color drained from Jake's face completely. "Are you saying that my grandmother's ghost told you that Russell . . ."

"Yes, I am saying that, with Inez's permission."

"Russell?" His fists clenched tight.

"It's true, Jake. It just seemed fair that you know so that you can close that part of your life and get on with . . . the next part. Inez felt it would free you to know. Did you never suspect it was him?"

Jake's eyes blazed with anger. "After it happened, Russ came to me saying he was going to help catch the guy who ran off with my wife and then left the scene of the accident. He went on and on about how we'd find him no matter what, acting outraged over the whole thing and more sympathetic than I'd ever seen him. His behavior at the time convinced me it wasn't him."

"It was, though. Ask Inez yourself, if you'd like."

He buried his face in his hands. "My wife wrote me a note saying she was going to Denver with the man who loved her, and I never told anybody about that note."

"She told your grandmother."

This was the proof. He could pretend all he wanted that he hadn't seen the ghost of his grandmother, but he had. And he knew Dana was telling the truth.

"That's it!" he said, slamming his hand on the table. He rose and stomped toward the door. "I'll kill him!"

Dana tried to catch him. "Jake! Wait! What are you going to do? Russell is—"

He whirled suddenly, his eyes so filled with the fire of rage that Dana stood immobilized, afraid of his anger. What would he do when he saw his cousin? Russell—and probably Jake, too—was sure to get badly hurt. Jake needed time to calm down. Better if he didn't know Russell was going to show up here any moment.

Growling like a lion, Jake shot out of the front door. Dana stood dazed, listening to him start the engine of his pickup.

She came to suddenly. Jake deserved to know that Russ was coming—and she wanted Jake's protection. If Russell was scoundrel enough to have an affair with Jake's wife and bold enough to make a pass at her in his office yesterday, what might he try when they were alone?

She ran to stop Jake, but it was too late; his truck roared out of the drive at top speed. Dana walked back toward the house, dreading the meeting with Russell. Just as she stepped onto the porch, a black car rounded the curve. Because the road forked, Jake had probably not seen it.

Damn! She'd bungled this. Now what?

She would just have to tough it out with Russell; try to stall him until she got confirmation that the check was on its way.

Russell MacGuire's car pulled into the drive. Dana had the urge to step inside and close the door, but he had already seen her. From the open doorway she watched him get out of his car and wave a bottle.

"Hi," he said. "We need to make an honest try at being friends. Common interest at heart and all that sort of thing."

The bottle was wine. He was also carrying a folder under his arm. Dana forced herself not to back away from him as she motioned him in. The best thing was just to get this over with, try to make him leave as soon as possible.

In the kitchen Russell set the black folder on the table and opened the wine. Dana produced two glasses and watched him pour. He looked over at her and spilled a little. Dana mopped up the wine with a paper towel, thankful it was white wine, not red that had been spilled on the tablecloth.

"To friendship," Russell said, raising his glass.

Dana did her best to smile and wondered what Jake would do when he discovered Russ was not home. Would he come back? If the temper ran in the family, she might make Russell angry, too, in her haste to get him out of here.

"This visit is a gesture of good will," he said with a smile. "I'm willing to cancel the lien on your house. I've brought a document that will clear you of any debts to me."

She pretended to be impressed by his gesture. But she still didn't trust him.

"Why, Russell? That paper is worth over three thousand dollars to you."

"The money isn't important." He reached into the leather folder and drew out a lengthy document—several pages of very fine print.

"I assumed you were going to make me an offer to buy."

He smiled. "You made it pretty clear you won't sell, so I figured if you can't beat 'em, join 'em. I'd rather be your friend than your enemy. The money involved is minimal."

She sipped at her drink, beginning to feel more at ease, while reminding herself that she shouldn't. "Will you tell me why you wanted this property?"

"I like that meadow beside the river."

Dana studied his eyes and thought, *He's lying.*

Russell MacGuire began shuffling through the papers in his hand. "This is all just legal mumbo jumbo about liens and payments." He pointed to a line on the last page. "All you have to do is sign it here." He gulped the rest of his wine and poured himself another glass.

When Dana picked up the document, the small print blurred before her eyes. She blinked, but it only made the blurring worse. Two papers slid out of her hand onto the floor. When she bent to pick them up, her head spun so badly she nearly lost her balance, and the spinning wouldn't stop. *What the devil is the matter with me?*

It took some effort to sit upright again. Russell sat in silence, watching her closely. Light glinted on the rim of the wineglass between them, and suddenly she knew.

The wine! He had put something in the wine!

The mayor of Devil's Fork shoved the papers closer and offered her a pen. "Just sign it right there."

Although she was unable to read the page of fine print, Dana was not so drugged that she would sign a document she couldn't read. It might be a paper signing her property over to him, for all she knew! In fact, that was probably what it was!

She stalled, unable to think clearly. She had taken only a few sips of wine, so how, when he himself was drinking plenty of it, could that be? When he spilled the wine and she turned her back to get a towel, he must have put something in her glass.

"Well? Aren't you going to sign?"

"I can't read this."

"I admit it's small print, but I explained what it is."

The wooziness in her head was getting worse. "Damn you!" she muttered.

Russell kept smiling. "Is something wrong? Come on, Dana, hurry up and sign this so I can put the papers away and we can relax and enjoy the evening."

"I won't sign anything I can't read."

"What do you mean, you won't sign? This cancels the lien."

"I want to read it over first. I'll give it to you tomorrow."

Russell got to his feet. "If you don't sign this . . . I'm afraid I have to insist that you sign. I'm tired of playing polite games with you."

Dana's anger flared. She didn't have to take this from anyone, especially not from the likes of Russell MacGuire. "You are in no position to threaten me!" The words slurred slightly, but she could hear the strength in her voice.

Russell grabbed her wrist. "I've tried to be nice to you, Dana, but you're not being nice to me, and I don't like that. Believe me, you don't want me for an enemy."

Dana could hear the sound of her own heartbeat. She was terrified of what he might do if he didn't get what he wanted.

Suddenly Russell drew back and stared at the door. Dana turned. "Jake!"

Jake stood in the doorway staring at his cousin with such intense hatred blazing in his eyes that Russell was immobilized, squinting as if staring into bright sunlight.

Dana looked from one man to the other, her heart racing. There was no doubt—none whatever—about what Russell was seeing in his cousin's eyes. Jake knew about him and Caroline.

Neither man spoke; Russell backed away, frightened of Jake's rage. Dana's head was spinning and her vision was not perfectly clear, but she could feel the tension in the air.

"Don't lose your head, Jake," she pleaded.

Jake stared at his cousin, feeling Russell's betrayal throughout his whole body. The fury building in him was so hot and intense that perspiration formed on his forehead. He heard Dana's words and saw the concern in her eyes, and struggling to gain some control for her sake, he reached for the wineglass on the table—her glass, three-quarters full.

"Jake, no!" she shrieked, but not before he had swallowed the remainder of the drugged wine.

13

FRIGHTENED, DANA TOOK a step toward Jake, but he
waved her back. He lunged toward his cousin, but before he could reach him, his knees buckled. He caught
himself on the edge of the table, struggled for balance,
tried to get back on his feet and couldn't. Dana rushed
to him.

Russell saw his chance. He snatched up the document and bolted. His footsteps sounded through the
foyer, followed by the slam of the front door.

Jake slid to the floor, holding his head. "What the
hell?"

Dana grabbed his hands. "The wine was drugged!"

Not a terribly strong drug, she realized; the effects
were wearing off already, but then she had drunk only
a small amount. Jake had consumed three times as
much.

"Are you all right?"

"Everything is spinning. I can't get my balance." Jake
ran his hands through his hair. "Where is he?"

"He ran."

"Too cowardly to face me, is he?"

Dana shook him. "Jake, you have to get this drug out
of your system. I'm going to make some strong coffee."

Jake cursed, but made no attempt to get off the floor.
Dana's hands were shaking as she filled a mug with
water and set it in the microwave. As soon as it had

boiled, she dropped in a couple of heaping teaspoons of instant coffee. Jake cupped the mug with both hands propped on his knees and slurped loudly.

"The wine was drugged? Why?"

"I think he wanted me muddled enough to sign his document without scrutinizing it."

"What document?"

"Supposedly canceling the lien, but I expect it gave him rights to the house. I'm sure it was a desperate attempt to get this property. But why?"

Gulping coffee, Jake scowled. "He tried drugging you? Hell, I'll kill him for that! I thought I knew my cousin, but damn, all those years he was lying to me. All along he was the one she . . ." He set the mug on the floor and rubbed his chin. "My head is still spinning!"

"Keep drinking the coffee. Is it helping?"

"Yeah, I think so."

"Whatever drug it is takes hold quickly, then wears off pretty fast. I'm already getting over the dizziness."

Jake tried to struggle to his feet, failed, tried again, and finally was able to stand. "The coffee is doing the trick. It's so strong it kicks like a wild mule."

"Do you want to lie down?"

"No. I'm going after Russell and have this out with him."

"You can't go after him now. You can barely stand up."

"I'm okay. It's wearing off." He combed his hair with his fingers and began shuffling out of the kitchen.

She protested. "You surely don't intend to drive?"

"I can drive blindfolded."

"You can not! You'll kill yourself!"

He put his hands on her shoulders. "Don't you understand, Dana? The betrayal I feel? All those years of wondering?"

"But what's the hurry?"

"What he tried tonight—tricking you. Drugging you. Do you think I'm going to let him get away with hurting you? Maybe the old betrayal could wait another hour—but not *this!*" He pulled away and started down the hall.

She called after him, pleading, "You're too groggy to drive!"

"Fresh air will clear my head . . ."

Anger flooded her. Men weren't rational about this kind of thing, she thought. But then, how would *she* feel if someone she trusted had betrayed her?

Dana started to follow Jake down the hall, but he had already reached the front door. "I think I know where to find him," he said. He didn't even close the door behind him.

Dana walked back to the kitchen, worried and defeated, then was startled out of her gloomy thoughts by a strange sight: the curtains were moving as if blown by a breeze, and the window was closed! Then Jake's coffee cup suddenly rose from the table and crashed to the floor.

The ghosts! They were frantically trying to get her attention! Fumbling in her pocket, Dana found the eyeglasses. The ladies were all chattering at once and waving their arms.

"You must run out of here," Maude said. "Russell is back!"

"And he's very angry," wailed Rosella.

Louise moved forward. "He didn't leave!"

"What?" Dana's gaze followed Rosella's plump finger, which was pointing at the ceiling.

"I'm afraid of what he'll do," Inez interjected sadly. "He doesn't handle himself well when his plans backfire. I'm afraid if he finds you alone . . . Well, don't let him. Just leave!"

Dana gazed toward the hall. "He isn't back."

Maude said impatiently, "He circled around to the garage and found a ladder. This very moment he's propping it against an upstairs window. He plans to climb into the house."

"And sneak down the stairs after you!" Rosella finished.

"Please get out of here. Try to catch Jake!" Inez pleaded.

Dana pulled off the glasses and ran toward the front door. Jake was starting the loud engine of his pickup. He couldn't hear her shouts.

She trusted the ghosts. If they believed she must get away from Russell for her safety, then it was true. She could get her car out of the garage, but her keys were in the house and maybe by this time, Russell was, too.

She yelled louder and ran toward the truck, but she didn't think Jake could see or hear her. Suddenly the truck jerked sharply into reverse and spun back. She waved her arms. A second later the truck slammed into the ladder propped against the side of the house. Russell was on the top rung.

The ladder began to sway. Russell let out a terrified wail and held on with both arms. The ladder swayed back and forth as if in slow motion. Russell had no choice but to ride it, hanging in the wind, pitching back and forth.

Jake felt the impact, light as it was. He opened the door, looked back to see what he had hit, then leapt out of the truck. He stood with his mouth open watching the ladder's dance and Russell, suspended in the air and hanging on desperately.

Jake jumped into the back of his truck, caught the falling ladder and managed to slow its momentum. It fell onto the roof of the cab, and Russell landed with a bounce in the bed of the truck.

Dana screamed and clapped her hands over her mouth. The mayor had landed, apparently unhurt, at the foot of the man he had betrayed. Jake stood over him, legs apart, hands on his hips, and didn't offer to help his cousin up. Russell struggled to his feet, holding his arm in pain. Without a word, he started to get off the truck.

Jake jerked him back. "Where do you think you're going? We have something to settle."

"Like what?" Russell rubbed his arm.

"The fact that you've spent seven or eight years lying to me."

"About what?" There was desperation in Russell's voice.

"You know damned well what. Your affair with my wife!"

"You can't prove that."

"Your actions tonight are all the proof I need. You were smart to try to get out of my way!"

Russell held his hands defensively in front of him. "You have no proof."

Jake jabbed Russell's shoulder with his fist. His voice lowered to a growl. "I have proof that you tried to trick Dana into signing a document by drugging her."

"I only wanted her signature."

"On what? You might as well tell me. I'll find out."

Russell wiped his mouth nervously. "I wanted the property. I have a right to it because of that lien."

"Why do you want it that bad?"

"It has a good meadow—"

Jake grabbed his cousin by the collar and yanked him right next to his face. "I asked why you want this property and I'd better get an answer."

Russell tried to push him away. "All right. You'll find out soon enough, anyhow. The county wants the land to build a new fairground. It's no big deal."

Jake maintained his grip on his cousin's collar. "It's a very big deal and you know it! Whether the land is sold or leased, there's a sizable profit to be made. Withholding that information is illegal as hell, and trying to cheat Dana and harming her in the process—"

"I didn't harm her!" Russell interrupted frantically, trying to pull out of his cousin's grip.

"Drugging her isn't harm?"

"Now wait—"

"I've waited too long already!"

Russell backed up. "I'm not going to fight you. I've got an injured arm."

Jake felt elation at having cornered the man who had betrayed him and a blessed release from the pain and confusion of past unfinished business. But his anger had not lessened, and he suddenly realized that his rage had far less to do with Caroline than with Dana!

Dana was his love. All that mattered to him now. And no man was going to get away with trying to hurt her.

Jake could hear her pleas now not to do anything crazy. Russell disgusted him. As much as he wanted to knock him senseless, concern for Dana stopped him— concern and love. She had been through enough. He wanted to tell her he had the thirty thousand dollars. He snarled, "Get the hell out of here, Russell. But I'm warning you, this isn't over yet."

Russell rubbed the arm again. "What do you plan to do?"

"Get you out of office for one thing."

"Ha! It's your word against mine!"

The stupid remark did not deserve a response. "Get off my truck. Be glad you're alive. You're lucky you weren't killed, trying to break into Dana's house with that idiotic ladder maneuver."

"I wasn't . . ." Russell began, then gave up. Moaning with the aches of his fall, he climbed slowly off the truck and limped to his car.

Dana sighed in relief. She, too, had noticed that tonight Jake's rage was directed less at Russell's affair with Caroline than at his treatment of *her*. It was all the proof she needed that Jake was not living in the past. He was thinking about the present and his love for her. She had been wrong and worried for nothing. Now she could give Jake the news that she was staying.

Together they watched until the black car had disappeared around the bend of the road. Jake stood at Dana's side, an arm around her waist. She said softly, "I can't believe you sent him off without a physical confrontation."

"He had a pretty bruising physical confrontation with my pickup."

He was breathing heavily, but the tone of his voice was casual. "But you didn't say that much to him, after all these years of wondering about your wife."

Jake looked down at her. "I haven't had a wife for a long time. It hit me when I was confronting Russell that it didn't matter anymore. I realized I have today to think about—and tomorrow. The past was a long time ago."

Words of freedom! Dana's instincts and those of his grandmother had been right. Learning the truth had set him free. It was hard to hold back tears of joy.

He asked, "Are you okay?"

"Yes. Are you?"

"Yeah, the adrenaline took the drug whoozies away real fast."

She sighed happily. "What happens now?"

He winced. "Damn, that paper he wanted you to sign. I meant to get it out of his car."

"I got it," she said. "I ran over and grabbed it. It's right here under my arm. I'm anxious to see what it says."

"I don't think there's much question about what it says. You heard him, about the fairground?"

She smiled. "Yes. What great news! But, fair or no fair, they can't tear down the house." She snuggled against his warm body. "Let's go inside. I have something to tell you."

"Something *else?*" He laughed. "I have something to tell you, too, but I don't want to go inside."

"Oh? You're not afraid of ghosts, are you?"

"To quote you, I don't like the idea of being spied on by ghosts. Besides, I made a fool of myself in front of the entire Ladies' club, and I'd just as soon not have to deal with them right now."

"Let's sit in the porch swing, then."

The swing creaked as they moved. Crickets sang in the grass and a locust hummed in the nearby maple tree. The moon was rising full and bright over the trees and the flowering honeysuckle perfumed the air. Jake sat with his arm around her.

Dana said, "Me first. I can't wait. I'm going to stay, Jake. In Devil's Fork. I've managed to sell my building in Dallas—where my shop was and where I lived—and I'm expecting the check tomorrow or the next day to pay off the taxes in full. And Russell's damn lien. The house will be clear, and I can live in it—with the adorable ghosts—and I'm going to start a small photo studio in town. In fact, I have my eye on an empty store already."

He fell into a heavy silence.

Uncomfortably she asked, "Did you hear me, Jake? I said I'm going to stay."

"I heard," he answered dully.

Fear coursed through her. Could she have been right the first time? Surely not after the way he'd been talking! "What's the matter? Aren't you pleased? I thought you'd be happy."

Jake looked at the rising moon, not at her. "Why didn't you tell me this sooner?"

Her heart felt heavy. The moist air blowing in from the river was suddenly hard to breathe. "I suppose I should have yesterday. There were so many things going on. I . . . I wasn't sure whether or not you would be happy about my staying."

His gaze swung to her. "What does that mean?"

"It means I was..." She swallowed, wondering what was going on with him. He *wasn't* happy with the news—at least, he sure didn't act like he was. "It means I was insecure about your feelings, I guess. I was afraid you'd feel pressured if I was a permanent resident here."

Jake frowned. "What you're saying makes no sense, Dana."

She looked at him. "How you're acting right now makes no sense. You act almost angry."

"I guess I am. Not that you're staying, but because you didn't tell me."

"Maybe I should have, but I can't see why a day or two makes so much difference. I'm telling you now. Why are you so touchy about it?" Her worst nightmare was coming true.

Jake shifted in the swing. He no longer had his arm around her, and his body was stiff. "It would have saved me a hell of a lot of trouble if I'd known. I spent half of yesterday morning—" He stopped abruptly. It had been difficult trying to borrow money without giving any explanation of why he wanted it, and the experience at the bank had not been pleasant. But why should he whine about that to Dana? Evidently getting the money had been a snap for her; she hadn't even had to make a trip to Dallas to do it.

To think he had been so excited about pleasing her with his solution to her problem—which he had believed was the *only* solution—made him feel foolish. Damn. She should have told him.

"You spent yesterday morning where?" Dana was asking.

"Never mind," he said.

"Jake, what's the matter with you?"

"Nothing's the matter with me," he replied. He knew he was like a little boy in a sulk and wasn't proud of it, but his pride had been wounded.

He rose. "If you want to give me that document of Russell's, I'll go over it to see if I can make a criminal case. It won't be easy to get him to resign from office, but he has to for the good of the town." His voice was flat and cold.

Confused by the change in Jake, Dana handed him the document.

"I'll look this over. See you later." He started down the porch steps.

She was near tears. "You're leaving? Jake, why? What are you so mad about? It can't be because I delayed one day telling you!" Tears filled her eyes. "You didn't expect me to stay, and now that I am, you don't know how to deal with it because you don't want me to get any ideas about commitment. You're *disappointed* I'm staying, aren't you?"

Hearing the tears in her voice, Jake turned around. He gazed at her for some moments before he answered,

"No, Dana, I'm not disappointed you're staying. What kind of sense would that make? I wanted— want—you to stay. It's just that I misunderstood your situation. You said you had no money for the taxes, and now suddenly you do."

Her heart was near breaking. "By selling my building, yes. Is that so bad?"

"No. It's just that I didn't . . ." He shook his head. "I took out a loan yesterday to pay your debt because I thought it was the only way to save your house."

She gasped. "You did what?"

"I was trying to help. You seemed so desperate."

She wanted to throw her arms around him and tell him how much she loved him, but the resentment in his voice formed a wall between them.

Jake thrust his hands into his pockets. "I talked myself into believing that the main reason you wanted to stay was me. Male ego at work, huh? I had no idea it was because a bunch of ghosts decided they wanted that particular house to haunt."

"Jake...I can't tell you how much it means to me that you wanted to help me."

"Then don't try."

"Please don't be angry. You *are* a very big part of my decision to stay, and you know it. You have to know it."

He stepped off the porch steps onto the grass. "This isn't the best time to talk about it, Dana. I've had one too many shocks tonight. I need some time to get my thoughts together. See you tomorrow."

The way he said it, she suspected she would not see him tomorrow. Stung because he did not even kiss her good-night, Dana watched him pull out of the drive.

She stood on the porch with the moon rising naked and lonely in the sky, casting its brazen silver light across the river and the meadow. It should have been their moon tonight, not cold and cheerless, but welcoming—a lantern for lovers to walk under.

When she went into the house and put on the eyeglasses, the dejected ghosts were waiting.

"Not good at all," Inez said sadly.

Dana looked from one to the other. "You all heard?"

"Everything." Inez shook her head. "It will be hard for him to have to cancel that loan. Jake likes to feel in control. That's the trouble with men, especially men like him."

"It's a guy thing," Rosella agreed. "He wanted to help you and you did better at helping yourself. That's a hard blow."

"Well, he's unreasonable," Dana argued. "I hate it when men sulk." She put on the tea kettle. "Oh, I should be understanding. I'm sure Jake was looking forward to my being so happy about his help, and I pulled the rug out from under him. I do understand. But what if he doesn't get over it?"

"We'll just have to make sure he does," Frances said.

"Yes, Dana needs our help," agreed Louise.

"Think, girls!" This, of course, from Maude.

Dana forced a smile. "I don't believe there's anything you can do about this one." She adjusted the glasses on her nose and sat at the table. "It's just as well, anyway. I mean, if Jake ever *did* to ask me to marry him, he'd expect me to live in his house, not here. I can't move from here and let this place go to ruin. To keep it empty would be awkward and expensive, and people would think I was crazy. I need to be here—live here—not at Jake's, so I don't see how I could marry him even if he asked me, which he probably won't, anyway. Not now."

A painful silence fell over the group. "We can't ask you to give up everything in order to live here," her great-aunt said.

Dana tried to lighten the tone of her voice. "It probably won't ever come to a decision, anyhow. Jake thinks I'm deceitful and—"

"No!" Louise wailed. "You can live with Jake. You must! He is the man you love, and he loves you. He proved that tonight. We will not ask you to give him up just because we need this house. Let it stand empty! We don't care, as long as it's standing."

Sighing, Dana rose to fix herself a cup of orange-pekoe tea. She said. "You all are wonderful. Should it ever come to that, yes, we will think of something. Right now, where I live isn't an issue. Jake thinks I don't love him enough." She stirred in sugar. "Darn! How can I convince him how much I love him when he's putting up that wall?"

"Think, girls!" Maude repeated.

"He needs time to cool down first," Rosella reasoned.

Evelyn sighed. "If he would just come here and Inez could talk to him—or maybe even all of us could talk to him."

"And tell him what?" Dana asked.

"Tell him how wonderful you are."

She laughed and shook her head.

Frances circled the table, asking, "What is this about a fairground? Can you sell the property for a fairground?"

"Not if the house is in the way. I'd only sell if I could keep the house, and it would be right in the middle of the fairground—" Dana flipped a spoon and sent it flying. She raised one arm with a whoop. "Wait! That's it! The house would be *part* of the fairground! I could make a museum out of it—a woman's historical museum, with all of Maude's beautiful antiques, and I could gradually acquire more! Yes! A woman's museum—dedicated to the Ladies' Club of Devil's Fork!"

"What a fantastic idea!" Frances exclaimed. "We could maintain the building with county funding!"

"I love it!" Dana said. "Don't you all love it?" She began to pace as the plan took shape in her brain. "I'd remain owner and manager and have my own quarters—perhaps even in the attic loft, which could be made into a fine room."

Rosella began to dance, and the others followed. The kitchen filled with whirling ghosts.

After a time, Inez stopped. "But wait. Why are you thinking of living quarters for yourself? We've agreed you're going to be Jake's wife."

"That might never happen." Dana remembered his eyes tonight when he left her and tried to ignore the pain that filled her. "I don't think Jake is interested in marriage. Especially now that he's mad at me. He's too darn touchy."

"Too darn proud," Inez added. "We must come up with a scheme."

"No scheme. He has to want me without any tricks, or it's no good."

"Do you love him or not?" Maude asked.

"Of course I love him. Too much."

She tried to ignore the fact that the ghosts were exchanging knowing glances. Something was going on, but she was in no mood for it. "Right now," she said, "I just want to get my mind off everything that's happened tonight. I'm keen on the idea of the museum, so I'm going to think about that and not Jake. I'll start the house inventory. That'll help get my mind off him." As if anything could, she thought with despair.

Maude liked this idea. "Why not begin in the attic? There are some wonderful things stored up there, especially clothes. I never got rid of the gowns and hats my mother used to wear."

Rosella twirled around and curtsied. "Oh, wouldn't it be fun to try some on?"

Frances scowled at her. "You can't try on clothes. You're a ghost."

"I didn't mean me, silly Fran. I meant Dana."

"Yes, it would be fun," Dana replied, intrigued by the idea of old trunks filled with turn-of-the-century clothes. She set the glasses on the table and hurried up the stairs.

No sooner had she found the attic overhead light and blown the dust from the lid of an old steamer trunk when she heard the phone ring. Her heart began to pound. It must be Jake! She flew down the two flights of steps to the kitchen and picked up the phone, out of breath.

"It's Nellie Jean," the caller said. "I just found out what happened! Lord in heaven, it's a wonder Russell isn't dead, with the ladder falling like that! Imagine him trying to trick you into signing your property away! It's a scandal of monumental proportions! Are you all right, Dana?"

How much does she know? Dana wondered, surprised. "It's been quite a night. But how the devil did you find out?"

Nellie Jean laughed, a rather wicked laugh. "Oh, you wouldn't believe. Donald and I were here in my office. I won't lie to you, Dana, I mean, I'm not ashamed of it. We were on the couch, smooching. It's sort of our place, where no one would find us after hours. Well, Russell *never* comes back to the office at night, but tonight he did. He was searching for something, going through files. Well, if he didn't look a mess! Like he'd been through a blender. He acted real funny and wouldn't say much, and after he left, I called Jake."

"You called Jake?"

"Well, Jake being the sheriff, I figured he'd know what had happened, and of course he did. He told me the county intends to make an offer on your property to build a fairground and Russ tried to trick you into selling. He said Russell fell off a ladder. Can it be true?"

"Would the sheriff lie?"

"This is wild! Didn't I tell you Russ MacGuire is a sneaky louse? And, wow, what news about that fairground! Dana, I want to talk to you tomorrow. Can we do lunch?"

"Sure. Talk to me about what?"

"Well, here's the thing. We have to get Russell out of office. Jake agrees. He says we might be able to do it legally, if we can come up with some proof that he tried to force you to sign that paper, which is just your word against his, and you are, after all, a stranger. Jake says he can try to put together a case, but it's weak. It could take months, and meanwhile, Russ will be working on support from the good old boys around here. Jake said he'll endorse me for mayor, but the election is a year away. Impeach a mayor? The legal system is too slow and too chancy. And he won't resign—unless we can force him to."

"That's what you want to talk to me about?"

"To discuss it, yes. I want to know *exactly* what happened. Jake told me you're staying in Devil's Fork and that pleases me absolutely to *death!* So I thought—"

"You and Jake had a long conversation," Dana interrupted.

"He sounded odd, though. Tired and angry. He wants Russell out, which is the best news I've ever heard. I never imagined I could get *Jake's* backing!"

"I'll do whatever I can," Dana said. "But I don't know what I can do that Jake can't."

"I don't know either. But I know this much—you have imagination—like I do and like they did—the Ladies' Club I told you about. They ran this town with style. I guarantee you if those gals were still around, we'd get Russ out. They *always* got what they wanted. So you and I must put our heads together and *think*. There has to be a way. For the sake of this whole town. I'd be an excellent mayor."

"You will be," Dana said with a smile. That prospect was exciting. She liked Nellie Jean. Obviously Jake knew Russell was going to fight this all the way. It wasn't illegal to have an affair with another man's wife, and even if the scandal would ruin Russell, Jake wouldn't use it. He hadn't mentioned Caroline to Nellie Jean, and Dana was certain he never would. Russell was safe with the secret and probably knew it.

So all they had was Russell's behavior tonight, which he would deny categorically. It wasn't illegal to draw up a document, either. Jake was right; it was her word against his. The battle they faced wasn't easy.

"Meet me at Chef Lou's at twelve tomorrow. Meanwhile, try to think if there's anything about tonight you could use as proof. Go over everything with a fine-tooth comb. We'll do it, Dana. We'll get the corruption out of this town just like the Ladies' Club did before. What was done can be done again. We must either trick or impeach! Whichever is quicker."

"I'll be right in there to help with your election campaign, Nellie Jean. We'll discuss it all tomorrow."

She hung up and put on the eyeglasses. The ghosts were already chattering. "Campaign? Nellie Jean?"

"For mayor," Dana said. "She wants to find a way to get Russell out of office fast. And herself in."

Louise squealed with delight. "Nellie Jean Schrock as mayor! No wheeling-and-dealing, pocket-stuffing politicians!"

"Can she win?" Dana asked.

"Of course! No one will run against her if Jake doesn't back Russell, and he wouldn't now."

"But what about Russell's other friends in high places?"

"If he has any, we can take care of them," said Frances. "We're sure to have enough dirt on them to keep them out of the limelight. We have a file of information in our heads."

Rosella winked at Dana. "With your help, that is."

"As our spokesperson," smiled Maude. "Girls, we're back in business!"

"Devil's Fork is ours!" Rosella sang, and began to twirl.

"Not so fast!" Dana raised her arm. "This celebration is premature. Nellie Jean talked with Jake just now, and he says getting Russell out will be extremely difficult. We have no concrete proof that he broke any law, and he will insist I'm lying. People know him and not me. The only hope, aside from spending months trying to build a case, is to convince him to resign. And Russell is not the resigning type."

"It's true," Inez agreed. "He's a fighter. He won't quit."

"Oh, my," said Louise dejectedly. "What can be done, then?"

Dana looked from one to the other. "I wish all of you could have heard what Nellie Jean said on the phone just now—about your club."

"We know how Nellie Jean feels." Maude smiled. "I had many conversations with Nellie Jean."

Frances nodded. "If she were older, she'd be one of us."

"She admires your tactics," Dana said. "The way you ladies always got what you wanted—and always for the good of the town."

"I admire our tactics, too." Rosella grinned.

Dana raised her arms. "Then let's use them! You all know what I'm talking about. The secret! Can we use it to make Russell resign?"

The ghosts exchanged glances. Maude began to laugh, then Louise, and then all of them were laughing, and the ghost laughter sounded like a thousand buzzing bees.

What was so funny? Dana wondered uneasily.

Evelyn spoke first. "Yes. It could make Russell resign—if he knew."

The buzz of laughter began again. Exasperated, Dana felt like banging her fist on the table and yelling, *What is the damn secret?*

Instead, she reminded them in a thin voice, "If it will affect Russell, then I have to know. You all agreed I'm one of you, and you want Nellie Jean to run Devil's Fork. So can you please quit stalling and just *tell* me?"

Frances slowly raised her right hand, followed by Inez and then the others. A unanimous vote. "All right," Inez said. "Lean in close, Dana. The only other persons who knew the secret took it to their graves. You are about to become the only living soul who knows. What you do with it . . . well, we'll have to leave that dangerous decision up to you."

DANA HOWLED with laughter. Tears streamed down her cheeks and she grabbed at the hem of the kitchen tablecloth to wipe her eyes. "It *can't* be!" she shrieked. "Omigod!" She held her sides and dissolved again.

"It's a devastating secret!" Maude said, but she, too, was laughing. Now they all were.

"Russell couldn't handle this," Dana said, choking.

"The *town* couldn't," Louise said.

Dana's thoughts began whirling. Should she go to Nellie Jean? No, not Nellie Jean. Jake. Giggling, she said to the ghosts, "Jake will know what to do with this. Agreed?"

They nodded in unison. They had known she would take their carefully guarded secret to Jake; they'd planned on it.

"I can't sit on this another minute," Dana said. "I'm going now."

It wasn't easy to drive. She was struck by fits of laughter as she drove, and her car swerved back and forth on the road. She wiped at her tears with a tissue and smeared her mascara all over her face, but she couldn't be concerned about mascara at a time like this.

Lights were on in Jake's house. Thank God. Her hands shook and her stomach hurt and her eyes were running as she rang his bell.

The porch light flicked on. Jake opened the door and drew a sharp breath, shocked.

"Dana! What's wrong?"

"Oh, Jake—"

He reached out and quickly pulled her in, as if from some danger lurking outside. "What is it? Are you hurt?"

She shook her head. "I had to come. I—"

"You've been crying! Oh damn..." He closed his arms around her and held her, and felt her chest heaving against his. "I'm so sorry, Dana. I acted like a heel."

He shut the door and led her by the hand into his kitchen, where he found a paper napkin and began wiping the tears and mascara from her cheeks. At one point, she convulsed again.

"Honey, don't cry."

She tried to say, *I'm not crying!* and couldn't. Instead, she took the napkin from him and blew her nose.

"It's okay," Jake said gently. "I've been sitting here thinking about tonight. About the way I reacted— overreacted. There was no call for rushing off like that, and I'm sorry."

She nodded, holding the napkin to her nose.

Jake kissed her cheek. "I was going to come back over and tell you I'm sorry. In fact, I was about to leave. I'm glad you're staying. I said I love you and I meant it. Please stop crying. I can't stand to see you cry. I'm a cad."

She ran her fingers along the buttons of his shirt. "You're not a cad. I came because..." She dabbed at her eyes again. "Nellie Jean called me after she talked with you tonight. She's very concerned about getting Russell out of office." Her voice came in jerks.

He nodded impatiently. "So am I. But it has to be done."

"There might be a way," Dana said, struggling for composure. "The Ladies' Club told me something tonight...."

Jake held her shoulders, and looked into her eyes. "What about the Ladies' Club? What the devil is so funny?"

"The ghosts told me a secret they've guarded for decades. If it got out it would turn the town upside down and Russell would be disgraced. We can use it to get him to resign—if you think we dare." She giggled against his chest.

"Good God, Dana! What are you talking about?"

"It's about the founding of Devil's Fork, about Russell's special project—the Hero, Brutus."

Jake's grip on her shoulders tightened. "What about Brutus?"

"Brutus wasn't what... Brutus wasn't a hero dog. He was a hero pig!"

"*What?*"

"Jake, it's true. They have proof. They've known for more than fifty years!"

He stared. "Brutus was a *pig?*"

"I swear. He found the gold nugget when he was rooting in the mud."

Jake drew back. Laughter began to rumble deep in his chest, and in a moment it filled the kitchen. "There's proof?" he gasped, when he was able to catch his breath.

"Yes. Inez found papers owned by your ancestor Penrose."

Jake sat down, calculating the immensity of this. "Russell has been Brutus's biggest fan. His election motto was 'The Brutus candidate...DOGgedly

working for Devil's Fork.'" Jake roared again with
laughter. "Russell's greatest pride is that statue. It's a
monument to himself as much as to Brutus. Hell, he'll
be a laughingstock! People here hate pigs. He's mayor
of a town founded by a pig!"

Dana squeezed his hand excitedly. "Am I hearing the
word 'blackmail'?"

"Blackmail, pure and simple," Jake answered. "It'll
work. Russ would rather be dead than endure that kind
of ridicule."

Dana grinned. "Now we know what ammunition the
ladies of the club used on Devil's Fork to keep the town
fathers in line."

Jake pulled her close. "When I left your house, I
thought I couldn't take one more jolt. Now you come
with this." He hugged her. "Dana, can you be happy in
Devil's Fork?"

"I'm coming to love your crazy town, Jake."

"Can you be happy in Devil's Fork with me?"

His eyes searched hers. She blinked. "With you here?
Of course. Why wouldn't I be?"

"I said *with* me. Forever. Could you be happy as my
wife?"

The shock of Jake's unexpected proposal left Dana
groping for words. "Jake . . . we've known each other
such a short time."

"Long enough to know we love each other. You're the
woman I've sought all my life. You don't know how I
worried about your leaving and forgetting about me.
Now that I know you're staying, I want you with me—
always."

Dana threw her arms around his neck. "I could never
have forgotten about you, Jake. I love you!"

"Then marry me. Tell me you will."

"Yes! Yes, I will!"

He hugged her tight, lifted her off her feet and twirled her around. "I'm the luckiest man alive! I love you, Dana. We'll make a place for ourselves in this town. We'll be happy here, you'll see."

She touched his cheek gently. "I've found all my dreams here, Jake."

"Dreams—and ghosts. What will we do about your house?"

She took his hands in hers. "We have a wonderful plan to turn the house into a museum on the fairground and dedicate it to the ladies of the club. They'll have it all to themselves—at least at night."

"And I'll have you all to myself at night. Every night." He hugged her. "They'll be quiet, peaceful nights, full of love, Dana. No more nights like this one, ever."

She smiled softly. "Tonight was frightening and crazy and hilarious," she said, "and it's turned into the best night of my life."

Devil's Fork was home. Jake's promise of tomorrow was the fulfillment of her dreams.

Epilogue

A DOZEN DOGS named Brutus came with the townsfolk to celebrate the wedding of the sheriff of Devil's
Fork. Some people gathered on the shaded lawn of the
O'Connor house, whispering and waiting for the bride
and groom to appear. Dozens more, who were more
curious than frightened by recent tales of hauntings,
had ventured inside to witness the ceremony.

Mayor Schrock stood beside the bride. Only that
morning, Nellie Jean had been sworn in. Her first official act had been to announce the future opening of
the new Meadowlark County fairground. Her second
official act was to change the law against pigs as pets,
to allow for "housebroken pigs only."

There were whispers about Russell MacGuire's sudden resignation the previous month "to concentrate on
his business," and much speculation about why he had
left town just before his cousin's wedding. It was Deputy Fargo who stood at Jake's side.

But most of the gossip on the lawn that sunny day
was about the bride's stubborn determination to have
the wedding at her great-aunt's old house. No one had
been able to talk her out of it, not even Preacher Whitney, even though the church was considered the only
proper place for weddings in Devil's Fork.

Chairs were set up in the living room and fresh flowers adorned the tables. At the front of the room burned six bright candles, their flames flickering against the dark wall.

As the preacher strummed his guitar and sang a love song, Jake watched his bride cross the room, in the ivory-lace wedding gown that had been Maude's. The lace veil that fell over her head and shoulders created the illusion of mist.

He held out both arms to her as she approached his side and whispered, "Your beauty takes my breath away."

A hush fell over the room as the ceremony began. Dana barely heard the preacher's words; she was watching the candle flames move in a room with no breeze, and feeling love from the guests no one could see.

"...I pronounce you wife and husband from this moment on, through thick and thin, but mostly through meadows full of flowers and through nights of love," Donald said. "A kiss will seal your vows."

In the embrace of her husband, Dana heard music, soft and ethereal. She whispered, "They're here. Can you feel them?"

"All I feel is my love for you." Jake smiled. "But I'm glad they could be at our wedding."

"Our strange little family—with their blessings for us."

The six candles flickered in unison.

Dana and Jake stepped out onto the porch to cheers and barking and a rain of rice. What sounded like the sweet buzzing of bees in the summer twilight was, Dana knew, the sighs and the laughter of ghosts.

Once upon a time...

There was the best romance series in all the land—Temptation.

You loved the heroes of REBELS & ROGUES. Now discover the magic and fantasy of romance. *Pygmalion*, *Cinderella* and *Beauty and the Beast* have an enduring appeal—and are the inspiration for Temptation's exciting new yearlong miniseries, LOVERS & LEGENDS. Bestselling authors including Gina Wilkins, Glenda Sanders, JoAnn Ross and Tiffany White reweave these classic tales—with lots of sizzle! One book a month, LOVERS & LEGENDS continues in November 1993 with:

#465 NAUGHTY TALK
Tiffany White
(Sir Gawain)

Live the fantasy....

LL11

HARLEQUIN®

Temptation

HARLEQUIN®

Temptation®

NEW AUTHOR

THE VOICES OF
TOMORROW TODAY

Sensuous, bold, sometimes controversial,
Harlequin Temptation novels are stories of
women today—the attitudes, desires, lives and
language of the nineties.

The distinctive voices of our authors is the
hallmark of Temptation. We are proud to
announce two new voices are joining the
spectacular Temptation lineup.

**Kate Hoffman, *INDECENT EXPOSURE*,
#456, August 1993**

**Jennifer Crusie, *MANHUNTING*,
#463, October 1993**

Tune in to the hottest station on the romance
dial—Temptation!

HARLEQUIN®

Temptation®

FIRST-PERSON PERSONAL

Nothing is more intimate than first-person personal narration....

Two emotionally intense, intimate romances told in first person, in the tradition of Daphne du Maurier's *Rebecca* from bestselling author Janice Kaiser.

Recently widowed Allison Stephens travels to her husband's home to discover the truth about his death and finds herself caught up in a web of family secrets and betrayals. Even more dangerous is the passion ignited in her by the man her husband hated most—Dirk Granville.
BETRAYAL, Temptation #462, October 1993

P.I. Darcy Hunter is drawn into the life of Kyle Weston, the man who had been engaged to her deceased sister. Seeing him again sparks long-buried feelings of love and guilt. Working closely together on a case, their attraction escalates. But Darcy fears it is memories of her sister that Kyle is falling in love with.
DECEPTIONS, Temptation #466, November 1993

Each book tells you the heroine's compelling story in her own personal voice. Wherever Harlequin books are sold.

LIGHTS, CAMERA, ACTION!

Hollywood Dynasty

HARLEQUIN™ *Temptation*

The Kingstons are Hollywood—two generations of box-office legends in front of and behind the cameras. In this fast-paced world egos compete for the spotlight and intimate secrets make tabloid headlines. Gage—the cinematographer, Pierce—the actor and Claire—the producer struggle for success in an unpredictable business where a single film can make or break you.

By the time the credits roll, will they discover that the ultimate challenge is far more personal? Share the behind-the-scenes dreams and dramas in this blockbuster miniseries by Candace Schuler!

THE OTHER WOMAN, #451 (July 1993)
JUST ANOTHER PRETTY FACE, #459 (September 1993)
THE RIGHT DIRECTION, #467 (November 1993)

Coming soon to your favorite retail outlet.

1993 Keepsake

CHRISTMAS

Stories

Capture the spirit and romance of Christmas with KEEPSAKE CHRISTMAS STORIES, a collection of three stories by favorite historical authors. The perfect Christmas gift!

Don't miss these heartwarming stories, available in November wherever Harlequin books are sold:

ONCE UPON A CHRISTMAS by Curtiss Ann Matlock
A FAIRYTALE SEASON by Marianne Willman
TIDINGS OF JOY by Victoria Pade

ADD A TOUCH OF ROMANCE TO YOUR HOLIDAY SEASON WITH KEEPSAKE CHRISTMAS STORIES!

HX93

Fifty red-blooded, white-hot, true-blue hunks from every State in the Union!

Look for MEN MADE IN AMERICA! Written by some of our most poplar authors, these stories feature fifty of the strongest, sexiest men, each from a different state in the union!

Two titles available every other month at your favorite retail outlet.

In November, look for:

STRAIGHT FROM THE HEART by Barbara Delinsky (Connecticut)
AUTHOR'S CHOICE by Elizabeth August (Delaware)

In January, look for:

DREAM COME TRUE by Ann Major (Florida)
WAY OF THE WILLOW by Linda Shaw (Georgia)

You won't be able to resist MEN MADE IN AMERICA!